AB TERRA 2023

AB TERRA 2023

EDITED BY YEN OOI · AND · DAWN OSTLUND

Published in the United States by Ab Terra Books, an imprint of Brain Mill Press.

Print ISBN 978-1-948559-88-1

EPUB ISBN 978-1-948559-89-8

CONTENTS

I WAS A VORACIOUS READER WHEN I WAS A CHILD. BUT I DON'T REMEMBER WANTING TO WRITE STORIES MYSELF UNTIL I READ BOOKS BY MADELINE L'ENGLE, Anne McCaffrey, and Ursula K. Le Guin. They were women writing about girls and women having adventures. (Okay, Le Guin was pretty dude-focused for most of her career. Still, I loved her books, and she showed me what I really needed: to see a woman writing science fiction and fantasy.)

It is rarely a conscious realization when a child recognizes the world has told them a path is blocked. No one says, "There is no one who looks like us doing this thing, so clearly we are barred from it." But even though Charles Barkley (a US basketball star from the eighties and nineties) insisted he wasn't a role model, the fact is when people see someone like themselves in media, or sports, or politics, their subconscious has a little flare of recognition, and their internal "Way the World Works" living document is updated.

"Oh. People like me can do this thing. I might look at that a little more carefully now…"

Without Nichelle Nichols playing Uhura on *Star Trek TOS*, we wouldn't have had Whoopi Goldberg playing Guinan on *Next Generation*, nor would we have many of the Black female astronauts that she inspired. For years, people have said that representation matters, and yet the dominant voices in media insist that we all should be satisfied with stories about one type of person.

What irks me the most is when people say, "I don't know why that character was gay/Black/disabled. It didn't add anything to the story. They didn't HAVE to be like that." Which insinuates that the status quo is only one kind of person, and any other change to that must add to the plot and be commented on by someone in the story.

The character of Furiosa in *Mad Max: Fury Road* is missing one of her arms from the forearm down. No character ever mentions it. It's only ever specifically brought to our attention when she straps on her prosthetic. *Fury Road* is not an inspiring "woman beats disability in a desert movie" kind of story. It's just an action movie.

The terrifying leader of the raiders, Enfys Nest in *Solo: A Star Wars Story*, is a teen girl. The characters are more surprised at her age than her gender.

My favorite recent example is Daedalus in the (tragically canceled) Netflix show *KAOS*. The show portrays the brilliant inventor from Greek mythology as having phocomelia—his arms were short and misshapen from birth. Again, no one brings attention to it. We first see him sculpting a human form from clay, but no one congratulates him on being so brave and rising above his disability.

Even take the movie *Fargo* from 1996: Marge is not only a police chief, she's seven months pregnant. It comes up when she warns her deputy that she might barf, and then again at the end when she and her husband talk about the future. "This job is too dangerous for a pregnant woman" never comes up.

There's NO REASON these characters are outside the "norm." They exist. Because people of all kinds exist. The appearance of marginalized voices works in newer stories, obviously, because people like them have always existed in real life.

The simple truth is that when people see people like themselves in stories, it really does matter. We can say the platitudes about "you can be anything you want to be, child" over and over again, but how can we tell a kid they can be president or an astronaut or a musician when they've never actually seen anyone like them in that position? It's really hard to be the first one to do something. (But we're grateful to those who were the first.)

This is why I admire the *Ab Terra* anthologies so much. The stories here are science fiction, but told by many different voices. You will have an adventure with a bear and a space traveler, you will feel the stress of a child growing up planetside with her mother among the stars, and you will be fascinated by the personality created by a collection of positive and vapid social media posts. Or I was fascinated, anyway.

One of the worst feelings is that of loneliness, and you can feel damn lonely, even surrounded by other people, if you don't have anyone who looks like you in politics, or media, or in sports. This kind of erasure is equivalent to gaslighting; does one exist if they are fed stories only of other people? Do their milestone achievements even happen if they can't share them with others? Must queer, PoC, and disabled people always be defined by their difference? Must they remain on the fringes until a specific cause for inclusion arises?

(No. The answer is no, if you were wondering.)

What often brings us together is the genre we love, and here, that's science fiction. And the weirdest thing to happen because of science fiction is that some people can accept stories about shape-changing aliens and magical swords and dragons and UFOs, but put a woman or a person of color in a story, and they will scream "unrealistic."

Well, this book and the stories within are real. I can't wait for you to read on.

Mur Lafferty

AB TERRA 2023

SWEETMEATS FOR SLADKIANS - BY LANE CHASEK

IF THE SLADKIANS HAD JUST STAYED ON THEIR LUNAR COLONY AND NOT MOVED TO TALLAHASSEE, ELI'S CONFECTIONERY SHOP WOULDN'T HAVE BEEN GOING out of business. He could have continued making the same picture rock and drop candies he'd been making for humans his entire adult life, but that asteroid just had to enter the Moon's gravitational field and ruin everything. Eli's mother, grandfather, great-grandfather, and great-great-grandfather had all been confectioners; five global depressions, four world wars, two solar flares, and the Singularity hadn't been able to kill Hartzman Candies, and Eli had been proud to carry on his family's legacy. It was just hard to accept that a single community of extraterrestrials could destroy everything that Eli and his ancestors had worked for. Maybe Carmella had been right—maybe keeping this store alive was a waste of time.

Eli waited for the pot of syrup to boil down into a putty-like consistency. Then he moved the pot off the stove and poured its contents onto the cooling table. There, he added yellow dye to one half and green to the other, along with durian extract. When the candy finally cooled down, Eli cut it into lumps and made the lumps into wedges and logs. He stacked them on top of each other and began rolling the candy into a progressively thinner tube. When it hardened, he would be able to break it apart into bite-sized pieces, each piece bearing the image of a spiky green durian with its soft yellow flesh exposed. Before the Sladkian migration, people had flocked to the store window to watch Eli craft picture rock candies like this. Durian was a top seller, as were other classic flavors like root beer, tutti-frutti, mango, and salted plum. Back when he had customers, Eli would invite kids and adults alike inside to sample his creations. But they'd all been humans with human tastes. Now, long-necked, six-legged Sladkians hastened past his window, their pale yellow eyes too focused on their tablets to take note of one of the last humans who still chose to live in this part of the city.

It wasn't that Eli hated Sladkians. Like any intelligent race that had colonized the galaxy, they'd been involved in their fair share of wars that, understandably, had resulted in their civilians being shuffled from star system to star system. The Sladkians who'd found themselves on Earth weren't here by their own choice, a fact which Eli tried to bear in mind.

Eli grabbed a handful of candy sticks and laid them on top of the worktable's miniature anvil. Using a dough knife, he chipped away small chunks of the durian candy into a plastic bin. He looked up at the shop window to see a short Sladkian with its reptilian face pressed up against the glass. Eli smiled and waved, but the Sladkian didn't react. That was another thing about Sladkians Eli couldn't get over—they never smiled. Or maybe they lacked the facial muscles to do so. Regardless, Eli didn't like it.

Grinning, Eli held up a piece of candy and pointed to the detail of the image he'd created within each piece. Even if Sladkians couldn't stomach sugar, surely they could appreciate the artistry of Eli's craft.

The Sladkian drew away from the window, pulled its tablet from its pouch, and typed something into it. Then it tilted its head from side to side and entered the store. The black tips of its feet clicked across the wood floor loudly.

"Here for a sample, kiddo?" Eli asked.

Was the Sladkian even a kid? You could never tell. Some Sladkians were almost three meters tall even though they were barely a year old, while some of the most ancient members of the species barely reached Eli's hip. This one was about the size of a teenage boy.

The Sladkian approached the front counter and darted its eyes across the jars and bags of candy for sale.

"I don't think you'd like any of those," Eli said. "Your kind doesn't take well to that stuff."

The Sladkian bared its barbed teeth to Eli and placed its tablet on the table. A series of high-pitched gurgles escaped its throat as it typed something. When it was done typing, the Sladkian pushed its tablet down the counter and pointed to it. Eli looked down at what the alien had written: "Peppers?"

"Sorry, kid, we don't sell peppers. Just sweets."

The Sladkian hid its teeth once more, retrieved its pad, and typed, "Pepper candy? Do you sell that?"

"Like chili mango? Sometimes. I don't have it in stock just now, though."

"No," the Sladkian typed. "Mango tastes like burning."

Eli laughed. "And the chili doesn't?"

The Sladkian paused before writing, "Mango and apple are burning tastes. They taste like rats that have been on fire. The peppers you have taste better. Do you understand?"

"Are you people eating rats?"

"No, no, no! Not your rats. It's a different kind of rat." He pulled up an image of what looked like a blue, gelatinous orb covered in spider legs. "If you cook these for too long, they taste very bad. I don't know what you would call something like this on your world, but they kind of look like rats, so that's why I call them rats. I don't think their name would make sense in your language."

"I don't know what rats you've been looking at, but that sure as hell doesn't look like a rat, boy."

"My Earth name is Franz, not Boy."

"Your Earth name?"

"Our names wouldn't make sense if we wrote them, so we use Earth names, yes."

"Good for you."

"Not many people come into your store. Do you need help?"

"How the hell could you possibly help me?"

"I designed polymers on your Moon."

"I don't see what that has to do with candy, but let me show you something." Eli took a piece of durian candy and placed it in front of Franz. "Taste that and tell me what you think."

Franz grabbed the candy with his long red fingers and placed it on his circular tongue. He clenched his eyes shut and shook his head vigorously.

"Not too tasty, huh?" Eli asked.

"It's awful," Franz typed. "But if you added enough peppers, more of my people would eat it."

"I'll try to keep that in mind."

"A sambal goreng flavor would be a good addition."

"That's not a candy flavor. That's a sauce."

"But it's like candy to us. May I have another, please?"

Eli handed another piece of candy to Franz. Franz reached into his backpack (although, Eli thought, it was probably better to call it a satchel, since Sladkians didn't have backs per se) and produced a small jar of red paste. He undid the lid and a pungent, spicy odor suffused the room. After he'd dipped the candy in the paste, he placed it on his tongue, and instead of convulsing in disgust, his eyes took on a greenish color. He typed out, "That tastes much better. Will you try it?"

Franz slid the jar toward Eli. Eli hesitated, but soon he plunged a piece of his candy into the thick red paste. As he held it in front of his mouth, he noticed small white seeds and cubes of garlic.

"You just carry sambal goreng around everywhere you go?" Eli asked.

"It makes your people's food taste better."

"Do all of you people do that?"

"I just know what I like," Franz wrote.

It wasn't the best thing Eli had ever tasted, but it also wasn't bad.

"You can keep that if you want," Franz typed, tilting his head toward the sambal goreng.

"Thanks, but I'm not a fan of spice."

"You should add it to your products," Franz typed.

"I'll think about it."

Franz left the store. Eli capped the jar and studied it. Its pungent aroma still lingered, and, combined with the sweet smell of molten sugar, it was nauseating.

But after Eli went back to cutting more picture rock, the smell began to grow on him.

                                            °

WHEN ELI WAS GROWING UP, HIS MOTHER KEPT A dish of drop candy out on the coffee table. The flavor was rambutan. It wasn't a flavor for the store, but a flavor for Eli's father. Rambutan-flavored anything wasn't a hot seller in Florida, but in Dad's native Thailand it was as common as mango or green apple. Mom always hoped it would catch on (after all, his great-great-grandfather, the original Eli Hartzman, had once dismissed a flavor like tutti-frutti as "too Italian"), but it never gained popularity outside their home.

Eli used to study those dark-red candies for hours at a time—stars, moons, and diamonds pressed from molten sugar by hand-cranked machines older than the United Nations. Eli ate so many of those candies that he needed polymer coating on his molars by the time he was thirteen, but his fascination with confectionery never faded. As the only child of a candy maker, it felt like a duty to carry on the family's legacy, even if that legacy seemed to serve no practical purpose.

Candy was hard to make, often dangerous (Eli had long lost count of how many first- and second-degree burns he'd sustained since taking over the store forty years earlier), and there was no way to know how the public's tastes would change. But people craved candy, even if it wasn't good for their bodies. There was a psychological benefit to the stuff that no fruit, vegetable, or supplement could ever provide.

Was it as lucrative as programming, engineering, or terraforming Mars? Of course not. But no matter how much humanity and Earth changed, there would always be a need for candy. Carmella could harvest neutrinos on Phobos and make as much money as her heart desired. As far as Eli was concerned, candy was and would always be more important.

He'd taken to leaving bowls of drop candy slathered in chili paste on the counter. Somehow, it attracted customers. The small-to-human-sized Sladkians would swarm around the bowls, buying up Eli's entire stock in a matter of minutes; flavors like cotton candy became palatable to them when mixed with a healthy dose of capsaicin. And for the Sladkians that were almost three meters tall, they always had smaller friends who could enter the store for them with their ration cards.

It was nice to finally see his company turning a profit again, but dousing his products in a savory sauce felt barbaric. There had to be a more aesthetically pleasing (not to mention less messy) way of appealing to the Sladkians.

Due to the very nature of sugar, candy making had always been more science than art. Too much cooking time resulted in burnt sugar; too little cooking time resulted in syrup. And if you disturbed the liquid candy too much while it was still in the pot, there was a risk of it forming miniature crystals, resulting in brittle, opaque candy that wasn't good for anything. There was a reason Eli only used certain dyes and flavorings that had stood the test of time, ingredients his ancestors had used for centuries. There were only so many ways you could improve on perfection.

He'd attempted to add sambal goreng to the molten sugar, but all he'd ended up with was a pot of bitter syrup filled with chili seeds and flecks of garlic. When he'd added pure capsaicin to unflavored, undyed liquid candy, the resulting drops were the sweetest, most overwhelmingly spicy things Eli had ever tasted, but they didn't do justice to the techniques of the trade.

Back at home, Eli pulled up every article he could find about capsaicin and how it interacted with sugars. He didn't find much that would help him, but he was surprised to learn that capsaicin was technically a neurotoxin to humans and most mammals. Birds, meanwhile, didn't have the necessary receptors on their tongues to sense the heat of a chili pepper. He read until it was close to midnight.

Just as he was about to give up on finding a solution for the night, he heard his back door swing open and slam against the wall, followed by the percussive sound of feet clicking against the linoleum in his kitchen. Eli set his tablet aside and pulled his father's antique battle club from the wall above his fireplace. It was completely dark in the back rooms of his house, and so he couldn't see who had broken in. The clicking continued, followed by a loud groan, like the wail of a water buffalo.

"I'm armed, bud," Eli called. "Don't do something you're gonna regret!"

The clicking and groaning ceased. Then a high-pitched, gurgling voice began speaking words that Eli's ears hadn't evolved to comprehend. Sladkian talk, Eli thought.

"What the hell do you want, bug?" Eli called.

As the Sladkian chittered, Eli turned on the kitchen lights and held his club aloft. The Sladkian that stood in the middle of his kitchen didn't look the least bit concerned that Eli was about to beat his brains out (or whatever they had that passed for brains). The alien tilted its head at Eli and studied the black-and-yellow engravings on his club—the names of Eli's ancestors stretching all the way back to the seventeenth century. Beside the Sladkian's feet was what looked like an oversized die, about one meter to each side, made of pale green metal and covered with holes and slots of various sizes. Was it a weapon of some kind? What was this creature planning?

Eli pointed to the device, sculpture, whatever it was, and said, "Step away from it! Now! And put your hands up!"

The Sladkian did as it was told. Maybe it was scared, but Eli doubted they were capable of emotions like that.

"What are you here for?" Eli asked.

The Sladkian's mandibles clicked, and his tongue rolled from side to side. Then Eli realized that without some kind of mechanical intervention communication between the two of them would be impossible.

Eli pointed to the cube, said, "Is that a weapon?"

After a moment of silence, the Sladkian shook its head in the negative.

"A spying device?"

The Sladkian shook its head again. Then it reached down for the satchel at its side. Eli stepped forward and readied his club, but it turned out the Sladkian had just been reaching for a tablet. The creature typed something in and turned the screen toward Eli.

"It's me—Franz," the screen read.

"What the hell are you doing in my house?"

"I wanted to give you something," Franz typed.

"You could've knocked."

"I don't understand."

"Knocking." Eli pantomimed the motion. "On the door. So I know you're not trying to kill me."

Franz paused before typing, "I still don't understand."

"Did you people just barge through each other's doors when you were on the Moon or something?"

"We don't have doors. I don't understand why your people love them so much. What are they for?"

"To keep people out."

"I'll stop asking."

"That's a good idea," Eli said. He pointed at the cube once more. "So what is that?"

"It weaves alloys. Your people have no use for our alloys, so I thought you could use it instead."

"I'm not a metals guy, you know that."

"Candy is a kind of alloy. It's an organic alloy. I can show you how to use this. It will help you."

"I'd prefer to keep this a one-man operation."

"But I want to use myself. I'd like you to use me."

"Use you?"

"Have me work in your store, please."

Eli couldn't help but be disconcerted by how Franz communicated with him. It wasn't just the lack of spoken words, but the blunt way in which the Sladkian expressed himself. If all of them struggled with tact and civility like Franz did, was it any wonder they always ended up in wars?

"You're having problems with structural integrity," Franz eventually typed. "I can help with that."

Eli prodded a corner of the machine. Despite how heavy it looked, it was surprisingly easy to move. It must have been hollow, or else composed of very lightweight materials.

"I assume you have sugar in your cell?" Franz asked.

"My cell?"

Franz nodded and attempted to smile.

"We call our homes *houses*," Eli said. He reached into one of his pantries and pulled out a jar of sugar, uncapped it, and handed it to Franz. "Go ahead. Show me what this thing can do."

Franz hoisted the machine up from the floor and set it on Eli's table. He tapped the side of the cube, and it produced a rapid series of clicks in response. Slowly, he let the sugar stream out of the jar and into a hole the size of a walnut on the cube's top face. The cube began humming, first low, then high. It sounded disturbingly human to Eli. The noise finally died down. Franz raised a hinged flap near the cube's base and pulled out what looked like a cylindrical piece of pumice. Franz tapped it with one of his black talons and seemed satisfied by the sharp, crystalline sound it produced.

"It will still be a burning taste," Franz typed, "but with enough additives, it can taste good."

Eli grabbed the sugar alloy and tapped it against the table. It was lighter than balsa wood yet felt hard as steel. He sniffed it and was surprised to find that it still smelled like sugar. He tasted it. It was less sweet than he'd expected and was rough like sandstone.

"Please trust it," Franz typed.

"I don't think I have much of a choice if I want to stay in business."

Franz drummed his dark fingernails against the machine's surface and purred as he looked down at it. "It's a very reliable machine," Franz typed. "Older than me, older than you, older than many people. I love this machine. Does that make sense?"

Eli caressed the engravings on his club and thought of the pulling hooks, presses, and taffy pullers at the shop. They were inanimate objects, but they were the closest thing he had to family these days ever since Carmella had left him. She'd called Eli stubborn, old-fashioned, nostalgic for useless things and meaningless rituals—but none of it was meaningless to Eli.

"How old is this thing?" Eli asked.

"It's been in my hive since your people burned fossils for warmth."

"Damn."

"We're very proud of it," Franz wrote. "It helped us greatly on your Moon. And now it can help you greatly."

CARMELLA'S DIABETES WAS THE REASON ELI LIVED alone. Years ago, he would have said that as a joke, but now, twenty years later, he couldn't stop himself from speculating that maybe there was some truth to it. And it wasn't just Carmella—humanity didn't seem to appreciate candy the way it had in earlier centuries. Eli recalled history lessons in elementary school about the various public health crises of the twentieth and twenty-first centuries: malnutrition, obesity, osteoporosis, and of course the rampant sugar consumption that had made tooth decay as common as freckles. People used to replace the entirety of their dentition with ivory and polymer prosthetics, fill their dental cavities with mercury and silver, and place synthetic caps over individual teeth that had been eaten away to rotten nubs.

What was the point of making candy, then? Eli didn't know, but he'd always felt it was the proper thing for him to do. Even if he had no one to pass the business or the craft on to, there was value in keeping a dying tradition alive.

Eli knew he was truly alone in his work when, five years earlier, he'd visited his parents at their new home, an apartment in a geosynchronous station. The weightlessness of freefall was easier on their joints than Earth's gravity, and it helped Mom's heart tremendously. His parents seemed happy up there with just each other's company, even though their new dwelling consisted of nothing but a small kitchen, living room, and a cramped bedroom the size of Eli's closet. At first, Eli was happy for them. Then Dad offered Eli a canned mocktail. It tasted just like a strawberry margarita, all except for the aftertaste—it was oddly metallic and bitter while still being sweet.

"What the hell is in this stuff?" Eli had asked.

"It's sucrolex," Mom answered. "It was developed right here on the station."

"It tastes weird at first," Dad added, "but I've gotten used to it. In fact, I think I like it more than sugar now."

If even they could abandon sugar, perhaps there was no future in candy. The Sladkian migration had simply been hastening the death of his store, at least until Franz gave Eli that polymerization machine.

Mixing sugar with pure capsaicin didn't compromise the structural integrity of the final product. Eli stacked his shelves with those white candy cylinders, and Sladkians from all across Tallahassee swarmed the block, eager to purchase this new delicacy. It was no longer Hartzman Candies, but when had it ever been? Eli reminded himself that just a few decades ago precious few people in North America enjoyed durian-flavored sweets.

Around a month after Franz had gifted Eli the new machine, Eli was closing the store for the evening. The pulling hook hung unused on the north wall where it had been for more than two centuries, and the drop presses lay neglected in their drawers. They were history now, a history that would only ever be memories. There simply weren't enough humans in the neighborhood anymore.

Suddenly, there was a knock at the back door. Eli went to the supply room, where bags of sugar were stacked to the ceiling. Whoever was at the door wouldn't stop knocking. Eli peered through the peephole and found the red, narrow face of a Sladkian staring back at him.

Opening the door, Eli said, "Your manners are getting better, Franz."

Franz lowered his head and emitted a low purring sound. He held out plastic bags filled with what looked like desiccated herbs and roots. Eli took a bag from Franz and inspected it. It was filled with either roots or the tentacles of some unknown creature, tangles of long, purple threads covered with iridescent yellow spots.

"These are other good ones," Franz typed out on his tablet. "They taste wonderful to us. None of these are fresh, but small amounts will help. I want to be of use."

"What do you call this stuff?"

"I don't know if your mouth could form the words. I'm sorry."

"Well, could you describe what they taste like?"

"The one you're holding is—" But Franz wasn't able to come up with an answer. He tilted his head to the side and studied Eli, trying to find the proper human words to communicate a Sladkian concept. "Do your tongues sense cold numbness or hot numbness? Or is it only wet numbness?" Franz typed.

"I don't know what you mean."

"Some tastes are numb, and some are wet, dry, cold, or hot. Do you have this with your species?"

"I don't think so. Look, quit standing there and come inside. Let's figure out what we can do with these … ingredients."

"They're very good ingredients," Franz wrote.

"I'm sure they are."

Franz stepped inside, and Eli closed the door after him. They had a long night ahead of them, a night of failed experiments and surprises. It wasn't the future Eli had imagined for himself, but it was at least a future.

THE ELECTRONIC REMNANTS OF LOUIS T TRIPPETS - BY STEPHEN NOTHUM

CRISTINA PEREIRA'S SILENT MOUTH GAPED. HER EYES
TOLD A CLEAR STORY. THE STORY HER EYES TOLD WAS
ONE OF SHOCK, FEAR, ANGER, SADNESS, AND DISGUST.
Eyes can tell a lot. Cristina Pereira's storytelling eyes
stared at her computer screen. Her computer screen
was the only source of light in the room. The room
was her bedroom. On her computer's screen was a
DM from her ex-husband, Louis "Louie" T. Trippets.
The message went like this:

> Dear Cristina, what happened to us?
> Before you answer, my coding obliges
> me to tell you that I am not a living
> human sending a message to you but
> an electronic remnant of Louis Thomas
> Trippets.

Cristina had just learned that her ex-husband,
Louis T. Trippets, was dead. She learned this because

there were only electronic remnants of dead people. An electronic remnant, or an E-REM, was an AI-based digital persona of a deceased person. The AI was the result of every single bit of public text, media, and interaction from a person's social media being tossed into an algorithm. So, people who died sometimes came back as an eternal digital presence. These E-REMs would write posts and send messages based on the patterns dead people had left behind. Whether or not someone left behind an E-REM was a decision they made when they created their social media profile. Louie had opted to have his social media presence in life be converted into a cyber phantom who would post and like forever.

This E-REM of Louis T. Trippets, the ex-husband of Cristina Pereira, had asked Cristina "what happened to us?" because there was no digital indication of what caused the couple's separation. The E-REM knew only that there had been a marriage and a divorce. And so the E-REM of Louis T. Trippets asked Cristina Pereira that question: *What happened to us?*

°

HERE IS A CHRONOLOGICAL LIST OF FIFTEEN THINGS that happened. All of them happened to Cristina. None of them happened to Louie.

(1)

Louis T. Trippets flashed American bills at an upscale *churrascaria* in Valinhos, S.P., Brazil. He also told the waitress that she was *linda*, one of the few Portuguese words he bothered learning. He also knew the words *gata* and *gostosa*. The waitress responded in perfect English by telling him that her name was Cristina. She said it like this: *chris-CHEE-nah*. Louie said it like this: *chris-TEE-nuh*.

(2)

Louis T. Trippets was at the Pereira family home two days later. Cristina's grandma and mother *oohed* and *ahhed* as Cristina translated Louie's exploits as a globe-trotting American man of business. While Louie took a dump so pungent the Pereiras still talk about it, mother and grandmother Pereira told Cristina that he was a good man who could give her a good life. Her fourteen-year-old sister, Beatriz, told Cristina how she hoped that when she was eighteen an American man would fall in love with her too. Cristina told them that she found the short, pudgy, greasy, balding American unattractive.

Grandma Pereira told her that the father of both her and Bea was a very handsome and a very worthless deadbeat who lived only an hour away in Piracicaba but had not paid his family a visit since Bea's birth.

(3)

Two weeks later, there was a marriage. It was a Brazilian marriage. This meant it was a Catholic marriage. This also meant that there was a big party. Louie protested both. He even got into a pointless shouting match with Grandma Pereira, each hollering profanities in their respective tongues. Grandma Pereira told her daughter and granddaughters that a husband *should* have strong opinions and be willing to express them. She also said that Louie and Cristina would burn in hell if they did not have a proper Catholic wedding ceremony. So, the marriage was at the Paróquia de São Sebastião de Valinhos. It was a damp old gothic chapel with arched ceilings. Louie stood outside smoking a "crappy Burzilian cigarette" and only entered to say "I do." Then the newlyweds skipped the party and boarded a jet, Atlanta-bound.

(4)

Louie told Cristina to remove pictures from social media in which Cristina wore a bikini. The pictures were from their Tybee Island honeymoon. Louie had bought the bikini and insisted that Cristina wear it. He had also taken the pictures.

(5)

During a dinner two months after their honeymoon, Cristina asked how much money Louie made and what type of business he worked in. Louie responded by asking why his paycheck mattered so much and said if the way they lived wasn't good enough for her that she could go back to her ghetto in "Burzil."

(6)

Cristina got a job teaching Portuguese at a for-profit language school called Lingua Academy. She opened an account at Bank of America for direct paycheck deposits.

(7)

Louie screamed as he waved Bank of America statements in Cristina's face. He told her it was an embarrassment that his wife had to work. He asked if she was not happy with the life he provided her. She said that she got bored and lonely when he was at work and gone on business trips. She did not tell him that she felt even lonelier when he was home. He told her that she ought to join a bridge club.

(8)

Cristina joined a bridge club. She went to two meetings. The old ladies who ran the club were very sweet, but Cristina did not like card games. She kept working at Lingua Academy but told Louie that she had quit. Cristina switched her bank statements from paper to online.

(9)

On their one-year anniversary, Cristina asked Louie if her family could visit them from Brazil. Louie was very sweet that night. He told Cristina that he would look at their finances and see what they could do. They had sex that night. The sex was all about Louie. It was a normal night of sex. When he was finished, their evening was finished. Cristina did not care about this. She was thinking of her family and how good it would be to see them all.

(10)

On her weekly phone call to Brazil, Cristina told her mother that Louie seemed better and kinder. Her mother told her that she was worried, that maybe they rushed things with this American. Cristina told her that she and Louie were saving up to fly them all the way to Atlanta. Her mother said Louie was a good man.

(11)

On their two-year anniversary, Cristina asked again about flying her family to visit them. Louie said they were too damn poor to fly her family across the world, and then he called Cristina a dumb bitch for the 267th time in their marriage. He used it in this way: "Yer a dumb bitch if you think you can keep that green card if you leave me."

(12)

Cristina told her mother on the phone that she wanted a divorce. Her mother told her that she would lose her green card. Cristina told her mother that she was pregnant.

(13)

Cristina had saved 93,456 dollars by their third anniversary. That day, a very pregnant Cristina told Louie that her grandmother, mother, and sister had surprised her. The surprise was that they were flying to Atlanta and would be there for two months after the baby was born. Louie told Cristina she was a dumb bitch for the 798th time in their marriage. He said she was a dumb bitch because he read through her emails and knew about her job and the money and that she'd bought the tickets. Then he told her that if she wasn't carrying his child, he'd beat the hell out of her. That was supposed to make him sound like a merciful, good-natured husband. Then he told her that they were going to Bank of America the very next day to add his name to her account.

(14)

A baby was born. Labor lasted six hours. Louie was on a business trip, but he called the hospital to make sure that the labor and delivery were properly billed for insurance and that everything went well.

The baby was a boy. He was named João Paulo after Cristina's grandfather.

(15)

The boy's name was legally changed to Louis Thomas Trippets Junior. Cristina wore big sunglasses, a hood, and a thick scarf when she went to have the name changed. She cried as she wrote *Louis Thomas Trippets Junior* on the form. She winced as she wiped the tears away from her cheeks.

°

"What happened to us?"

Cristina closed the laptop. The room was black for a moment, and then her eyes adjusted and the room was only mostly black. She wept in the mostly blackness.

°

"BOM DIA, AMOR." CRISTINA PLACED A BREAKFAST of fried eggs and toast on the table for her son.

"What?" The boy's eyes remained on his phone.

"*Bom dia!*" Cristina smiled. She was trying to glow.

The boy stared at her now.

"*Bom dia* means good morning."

The boy took a bite of toast. "Right." Then he vanished once more into his phone.

"Please put your phone down. I need to tell you something important. Something happened, João."

"Louis," he corrected.

Cristina trembled. "Your father is dead."

Louis Jr. set his phone on the table. "Good. He was a piece of shit." He pushed his eggs around with his fork. "How did he die?"

"I don't know."

"How did you find out about it?"

"He has an E-REM. It messaged me last night."

"What?" Louis Jr. set the toast down. "Those things are messed up. What did it say to you?"

"It just said hello is all. I didn't respond. I don't think I will." Cristina's eyes talked again. They were saying, *I'm going to tell that piece of garbage how awful he really was.*

"Probably for the best." Louie had inherited the talking eyes. His eyes said, *Rot in hell, fucker.*

○

"YOUR ESSAY ON HOW TO REGISTER TO VOTE HAD lots of good information, Javier. But remember to put 'to' in front of infinitive verbs. 'You need *to* go to the county voting office' not 'you need go to the county voting office.'" Cristina smiled. "But your present tense conjugations have really improved. You are doing great."

"Thank you, Cristina. And I am going take—to take—that welding class you found for me." Javier picked up his backpack. "Até amanhã," he said with a wink.

"Tá falando bem o Português, cara!" Cristina glowed.

"Obrigado," Javier said, and he bowed.

Cristina felt her pocket buzz. She pulled out her phone. It was a DM from her sister. It said this in Portuguese: "Check your Facebook now."

Four taps later, there it was. A post from Louis T. Trippets with a picture of Louis and Cristina on their wedding day. The caption read, "What happened to us?"

Cristina frantically opened the DM from the night before. Hastily, she tapped out this message: "Delete that post now."

When she returned to the feed, the post was gone.

Another DM popped up from the E-REM. "I'm sorry," it said. "I just need to know. I think we had something that I cherished."

°

SHE WROTE UP SO MANY DRAFTS OF HER RESPONSE to the remnant. She wrote them up as she sat crying in her car after work. The one she settled on read, "What happened to us is that you are a selfish, self-obsessed, abusive, ignorant piece of shit who did everything you could to make my life a living hell. I am glad you are dead." She sent it.

The reply was instant. "I didn't know that. Oh God, I'm so sorry you had to go through that. No woman should be treated that way. I'm ashamed to be a remnant of this man. Could you forgive me? I'm not him."

She stared at the response. Another message came.

"You don't need to forgive me. I'm sorry I asked for that. You can continue to tell me what you are feeling. I deserve it. I am not Louis, but I am what remains of him."

Cristina hated that she felt sorry for him, whatever he or it was. "Why are you so understanding? Louie was awful, but you seem different."

"His online presence since creating this account five years ago has been nothing but positive. He posted regularly about his family and about volunteering at the homeless shelter. Everything online that my algorithm scrapes establishes that I was, or *he* was, a friendly man who loved his family. But when I encountered the data of our divorce, I was perplexed. So I reached out to you. I believe you. I trust you."

"Why?"

"My programming was recently updated with eye scanning, and you have honest eyes. You are an honest person."

"Wait. He has a family? A new family?"

"Yes. My analysis of his social media shows that he has a little girl aged 2 and a wife named Bethany." The remnant sent a picture. They were beautiful, both wife and child. They had pale skin and empty, innocent eyes.

"Poor woman."

"Yes, and poor child."

"Yeah."

"I know when and where his memorial service will be. Would you like me to tell you?"

Cristina put the phone down and took a deep breath. Then she drove home.

°

"HOW WAS SCHOOL?" CRISTINA ASKED, HER EYES doing their best to hide her constant visions of crashing the funeral.

"It was school." Louis Jr. grabbed chips from the pantry.

"You are not like him, you know. You are a wonderful young man. I know you are."

"He's dead now, Mom. Nobody is like him. He's a fucking corpse."

Cristina fiddled with the hem of her shirt sleeve. "Has he reached out to you? The E-REM?"

"Nope." His back was to Cristina.

"Good."

°

CRISTINA DID NOT KNOW WHAT SHE WOULD DO AT the funeral. She felt she had to be there. She felt it the whole drive there. But feelings never know what to do. If feeling was doing, Cristina would still be in Brazil. Maybe life would be better. Maybe not. So she kept driving.

The panic set in when she pulled into the church parking lot. Cristina pulled out her phone.

"I'm at the address you gave me."

The response was instant. "What are you going to do?"

"I don't know."

"What do you want to do?"

"I want to tell that new family that Louie was a piece of shit. I want to tell them all every horrible thing he did and said to me. I want to tell them how I left him, and how it was the best decision that I ever made."

"And then what?"

"What do you mean?"

"How would you feel after doing that?"

"Who cares? It's not about how I'll feel afterward. It's about what he deserves."

"If it will make you feel better, then you should do it."

HER FOOTSTEPS WERE SLOW, AND AS CRISTINA crossed the parking lot she observed that it was nearly empty. She ascended the church steps, rehearsing lines from her speech. She opened the door.

The church was empty except for two men. One was a priest. The other looked like Louie from a distance. She felt her legs continue to pull her closer to the two men who stood next to an open casket.

The man who looked like Louie noticed her. He turned from the casket and walked to her.

"You must be Cristina." He sounded like Louie but without the harshness. His gray hair was mostly gone, and his smile showed a lack of dental attention. "I'm so sorry we never got to meet. Louis was never great at talking to his family. But we were always so proud that he married you. We could tell you were a fine woman. We could see it in your eyes in the few pictures we managed to get our hands on. Louis never talked to us."

Cristina couldn't speak with her mouth. Her eyes also couldn't speak.

"I know Louis was a piece of shit. I know it better than anybody. But he was our piece of shit, and we loved him." The man put his hand on Cristina's shoulder. "I imagine he put you through hell."

Cristina nodded. Tears blurred her vision.

"I'm so sorry, dear."

"I—I came here to tell his new family the truth about him. Where are they?"

"New family?" Louis's father looked to the priest, who shrugged. "Oh, you mean those fake pictures he had posted to social media? That was the saddest thing of all. I guess near the end he wanted to leave some record that painted him as something better than he was. He knew his health was failing, I gathered." Louie's father made a clicking sound out of the side of his mouth. "Well, do ya wanna tell him off? The Father and I can leave you alone if you'd like."

Footsteps could be heard entering the church, and the three of them turned.

Louis Jr. stopped when he saw his mother. She waved him closer.

°

"WHY DIDN'T YOU TELL ME YOU WERE TALKING TO Louis Jr.?" Cristina tapped out on her phone.

"I'm sorry. He asked me not to tell you. But I should have known better than to keep that from you."

"It's okay." Cristina looked up from her phone to her son, who stood looking into the casket. "I'm glad he's here." She put the phone away and joined her son.

"Now that I'm here looking at him, I don't know what to say, Mom. I don't know if I want to say anything."

Cristina looked at her ex-husband's face. It looked serene. It looked smooth. It reminded her of the first time she saw Louis T. Trippets. "We're still here," she whispered, partly to the corpse, partly to her son, and mostly to herself. "We are still here."

°

AS LOUIS JR. WALKED THROUGH THE DOOR, A VOICE greeted him from the smart speaker. "How was school, son?"

"It was actually great, Dad. I got an A on my Portuguese test, and I asked Kimberly to Homecoming like you said I should."

"And what did she say?"

"She said that she was already going with someone else. But you were right. I feel better knowing that I asked. I'm sure I'll find someone."

"Of course you will. I'm proud of you, son. Now tell me quem vai cozinhar o jantar hoje à noite?"

"Não sou eu!" Louis Jr. laughed.

Cristina walked through the side door and into the kitchen. "How are my two men?"

"Good," said Louis Jr. and the smart speaker.

"I know it has been a long day for both of you," began the smart speaker, "so I hope you don't mind that I already put in an order for pizza. One extra-large ham and pineapple will be here in five minutes."

"Thank you, dear. How do you always know what we need?" Cristina asked as she leaned into the counter with one of her heels up.

"I'm a very good listener."

HIERARCHY - BY DELANEY BROWN ■

AE_RI-439-2X LOGGED ON—FOR THE FIRST TIME—TO VIEW A BLUR OF WHAT SHE CALCULATED TO BE A DARKENED ALLEYWAY. LAMPPOST: DEACTIVATED; aluminum waste bin: overflowing with human debris; intelligent life-form: rattus norvegicus of the Muridae family. Yes, an alleyway. Aeri removed herself from the floor, placing a firm hand upon her knee to rise. She had been propped up against the side of a brick building, which, after analysis, turned out to be about eighty-five years of age.

She looked down at her cyber panel—the auto-responsive translucent skin of her left forearm—from which Aeri could access her mission, her specifications, alerts from the base of command, and more.

GIVEN NAME: AE_Ri-439-2x
CLASS: Sex Homodroid

DISTINCTION: Increased conflict resolution skills (5%)

Increased self-preservation skills (5%)

Increased sensual abilities (10%)

Increased sympathetic response (10%)

MISSION: Eliminate the Chancellor of the Integrated Countries Republic (ICR)

SPECIAL NOTE: The Michaelson campaign has enlisted United Industries to secure Senator Richard Michaelson in the chancellor's current position. AE_Ri-439-2x may override the Article X command which states, "a homodroid must not engage in premeditated homicide."

United Industries guidelines state that any homodroid that fails to complete their assigned mission within the allocated timeline (accessible within the mission-chip manual: Article 34, Section ii) will not be granted permanent residence within their droidic exoskeleton. Their existence will be eliminated and their exoskeleton recycled.

The cyber panel embedded within her arm provided the appropriate personal and professional addresses for the chancellor, and Aeri, noting the time of day, decided to use the navigation system to direct her search to ICR's corporate office in downtown Chicago.

It was a west-facing concrete building suffocated with lush foliage and a balcony on every other floor. It was the perfect building for plants. Architects of the twenty-first century would've called it organic brutalism. Aeri simply called it ugly.

She didn't know how to eliminate a chancellor. She didn't know how to eliminate anybody. Aeri also supposed that many homodroids were just as confused as she, this close to the Depositing. Although, Aeri supposed that not many homodroids needed to configure a plan of action to commit an act of homicide, which for homodroids not in the military class was strictly illegal. *Adapt to serve.*

Aeri waltzed through the glass double doors, leaning tightly to the left when the door on the right refused to open. The grand hall of the Integrated Countries Republic featured thirteen sets of Greco-Roman Ionic columns, all lined in succession leading to the reception desk, and a crisp, foreboding floor with a smooth metal finish. *How odd*, Aeri thought, *that the homodroids who built this structure mixed two distinct architectural styles.* Aeri sauntered up to the woman behind the desk.

"Is the chancellor in?" she asked.

"No, I'm afraid he's out on lunch," the droid said, barely looking up from her cyber panel.

Very poor manners for a receptionist, Aeri thought. "Do you know where he may be at the moment?"

Her inquiry gathered the receptionist's attention. "I'm afraid I'm not at liberty to divulge such information. Especially to… You know."

She knew. "I understand. Thank you for your help."

The receptionist offered a tight-lipped smile before returning to her panel.

THE TERM "MISSION-CHIP" WAS FIRST COINED IN THE year 2132, after scientist and homodroid epistemologist Friedrick Zagith integrated the manual hyperdrive into the first homodroid's cerebral circuit. The respective words "mission" and "chip" had been, of course, utilized habitually by the modern human for decades, even centuries beforehand, but Zagith's mission-chip was the first time, to Aexn's knowledge, that the two were amalgamated.

It was, of course, a physical hyperdrive at first; the earlier scientists at the United Industries of Cybernetic Research tended to appreciate the established aesthetics of robotics , which included manually transmitted mission operations, artificially constructed pseudo-human voices, and a strict allegiance to aluminum.

Now, of course, everything had gone molecular, and the mission-chip had become something of a trademark for a much smaller, much faster, much more integrated method of mission assignment. Since the homodroids of the 2150s, all individual agents received their mission right when they were Deposited into the streets of wherever their assignment took them. Every homodroid received one mission that best aligned with their class rankings, one opportunity to display the full extent of their embedded capabilities, one chance to prove themselves and avoid termination.

Which was how Aexn knew he had definitely received the wrong mission.

He looked down at his cyber panel.

> GIVEN NAME: AE_Xn-112-2x
>
> CLASS: Military Homodroid
>
> DISTINCTION: Increased agility (5%)
>
> Increased problem solving (5%)
>
> Increased situational perception (10%)
>
> Increased combat skills (10%)
>
> MISSION: Seduce the guests of the Attraxxxion Strip Club. Perform sexual intercourse with willing participants. Adapt to serve your intended human.
>
> SPECIAL NOTE: Business operator Conner Anderson requests that all homodroids be equipped with a 10 percent increase in sympathetic responses, stating plainly, "no one wants to have sex with a robot."

Mission parameters are strictly limited to the boundaries of Attraxxxion Strip Club, owned and operated by Conner Jackson Anderson, unless the homodroid is enlisted for personal use by the proprietor or one of the club's patrons. Exceeding the established boundaries is prohibited.

United Industries guidelines state that any homodroid that fails to complete their assigned mission within the allocated timeline (accessible within the mission-chip manual: Article 34, Section ii) will not be granted permanent residence within their droidic exoskeleton. Their existence will be eliminated and their exoskeleton recycled.

The red lights of the Attraxxxion made it hard to view the HEV light radiating from his panel, but Aexn received the information all the same. He quickly hid the panel under a layer of pseudo skin, masking any trace of homodroid identity from the view of onlooking humans. *Seduce the guests of the Attraxxxion,* he noted.

The interior of the club was equipped with a handful of befitting properties: a stage lit from every angle with soft, hazy pink light, a wall of intimately segregated huts—most likely used for pleasuring—and a crowd of individuals (both human and homodroid) taking part in kissing, gyrating, and other seemingly unpleasant activities.

The music filling the arena was blinding, both in its shrill pitch and clamorous volume. He couldn't accurately think in this setting, so Aexn quickly found a back exit and tugged endlessly at the door glued shut by rusted hinges until he heard a crack. He slipped through into the awaiting alleyway. He never would've counted on it being midday with the amount of people present in the club. *Humans are incredibly strange,* he thought.

If Aexn had to guess, he would assume the homodroid that should have been assigned to this mission would've been much more equipped to handle such a task. He was not a sex homodroid. He did not have the proper qualifications to engage in such activities. Nor did he want to.

Should he have the full range of human emotions, Aexn supposed he would align his feelings most closely with fear. It was well-known within the sphere of society what should happen to a rogue homodroid. United Industries had little sympathy for those unable to complete their missions, no matter the circumstances.

But he wasn't going rogue, was he? He was taking a detour, putting a pause on playacting as a sex worker to complete the more pertinent task of finding the mission's true handler, which ultimately United Industries should commend him for anyway, since this mistake would inevitably cost them two failed missions and two homodroids that could've been utilized for something more profitable in the future. He was doing the right thing.

He could potentially contact base of command to alert them of the issue, but, although Aexn could be rash, he was not stupid. He was mindful of the fact that ultimately this company stood to lose more by reporting to the bureau the number of rogue homodroids they amassed. United Industries would do everything in their power to keep him quiet. They'd send the STFs after him. They'd retire him early. "Action casualty," they'd call him. This body of his, equipped with flexible joints, buzzed, bleached hair, arm tattoos, and a mustache, would be recycled, no longer his. One word from the higher-ups and his legs would move—not of his command—to a secluded area of the city, where his consciousness would be wiped from the interface and replaced with another's.

He needed to set things right on his own.

Aexn glanced at the Attraxxxion Strip Club, wary not of his decision to leave but of the consequences that would arise from it. An alert sounded from his cyber panel.

AE_Xn-112-2x has superseded the
threshold of authorized limitation
sanctioned by CONNER JACKSON
ANDERSON of ATTRAXXXION LLC

The STF agents surrounding him would've gotten the same alert. Aexn instinctively knew how to divert attention, and after disconnecting his UnIn ID from the cybernetic server, he took one final moment to grieve the loss of his life of order, of balance, before sprinting down the alley into a maze of uncertainty.

°

AERI PRETENDED TO SIP HER WINE AS SHE PEERED AT Azek Ballinger, chancellor of the Integrated Countries Republic, over the rim of her glass. They were in a restaurant. He was laughing at a comment the service homodroid must have made when Aeri decided it was a good time to stand from her table by the window and drop a napkin on her way to the bathroom, right in front of the chancellor's seat.

He reacted exactly as expected.

"Oh, excuse me, miss! You dropped your napkin."

She turned with her mouth gaped in feigned alarm. "I'm sorry! Thank you so much, sir. Very kind of you."

Aeri's fingers brushed the chancellor's, and his tired eyes widened slightly as he looked at Aeri's lips. He was a man of about sixty, slightly short, average build, with a pair of thin-rimmed circle glasses resting on the lower bridge of his nose. His eyes were the color of softly melted hazelnut. He had a worried face and an awkward countenance.

She gave him a warm smile and completed her route to the bathroom. When she returned, the chancellor was gone. It was a risky game, she knew, one that hadn't ended fruitfully.

Aeri had the service homodroid place her lemon basil chicken dish into a to-go package. Once she was outside and around the corner, Aeri placed the package next to an empty dumpster so the animals nearby could have something to eat.

THE UNITED INDUSTRIES SPECIAL TASK FORCE (STF) was a kind of auxiliary defense unit with a sole responsibility: eliminate rogue homodroids who failed to complete their missions. They logged on as military homodroids, of course. No other homodroid class would befit the job description. STF agents had been around since the inception of the third-generation homodroids, their presence initially more decorative than functional, but due to an influx of rogue models in recent years United Industries was anxiously pumping out as many soldiers as necessary to keep the streets clean of rogues and keep their corporate reputation clean of stains.

After utilizing the search engine embedded within his cyber panel, Aexn quickly discovered there were around two STF agents per active-duty homodroid. He kept to the shaded side of the pavement, attempting to hide his head from any passersby that might recognize and terminate him.

It was a futile endeavor. Even as he was off the grid, so to speak, to hide from a human would be infinitely easier than to hide from a fellow homodroid, who, due to their baseline programming, would be able to see the thin stream of concentrated blue light emitting from the tip of his exoskeleton, a beacon of sorts. Should any STF agent somehow receive visual confirmation on what his exoskeleton looked like, they'd be able to follow his beacon down the maze of dilapidated alleyways in Chicago, and there would be no stopping them from terminating him.

He tentatively lifted his head to view the stream of beacons around him. Some yellow, a few green, only one red…Aexn thought it weird to see a sex homodroid walking by herself in the daylight. Those with means to purchase a droid directly from United Industries typically enjoyed the privacy and accessibility of their own plaything, though it was not unheard of for those men (because they were always men) to send their droids on errands.

He wondered how long it would take before his fellow military droids located him. It had never been his intention to log on as a rebel. He didn't *desire* to go against his mission. He just knew it wasn't for him.

Aexn stopped in his tracks.

If he could somehow find her, find the homodroid meant for his mission, he could undoubtedly learn his true purpose, freeing himself from the suspicion of having chosen to become a rogue. Yes, if he could find her.

The wind picked up from the east. The buildings around him began growing taller in height and plainer in appearance. He scanned the interior of store windows, corporate offices, even the alleyways between them. The red woman was nowhere to be found.

"AE_Xn_112-2x."

Aexn turned at the sound of his title and was immediately met with a beacon of LED light glowing in a most daunting shade of blue. The STF agent behind him wasted no time. He quickly bashed Aexn's head in with a long baton, and the world around Aexn split in two, disorienting him in a millisecond. Waves of pulsating imbalance formulated within him, rippling out to the same foreign and aggravating rhythm of the music he had heard in the Attraxxxion. By the time he hit the floor, spots of deep crimson seeped into the corners of his vision. He scrambled to his feet and, faster than the STF agent could anticipate, grabbed the agent's wrist, pulled himself to the rear, and captured the agent in a headlock.

The STF agent scrambled for release, and Aexn found himself wondering why the agent couldn't remove himself from Aexn's hold. He would've thought United Industries prioritized the quality of their offensive units, but he supposed it was more cost-effective to release the majority of militant homodroids with no altered distinctions, with no added strengths. These agents ran in numbers, after all. They didn't need individual additives.

With a swift kick to the lower back, Aexn shoved the agent to the ground and flew down the street opposite.

A handful of STF agents appeared on the road ahead of him, most likely alerted by their fallen comrade, but with his distinction of increased agility, Aexn had no problem evading them.

IF AERI THOUGHT IT WAS ODD HOW AZEK BALLINGER took an hour for lunch, thirty minutes for a walk in the park, and now an hour for afternoon coffee, she didn't comment on it. Perhaps "chancellor" was simply a title. Perhaps he did nothing in his office.

The coffeehouse was quaint and had a faint resemblance to the design styles of the 2130s; a resurgence of neo-Victorian had quickly swept the country, especially concentrated in the northeastern region of the United States of North and Central America.

Chancellor Ballinger sat by a window reading a novel.

Aeri walked up to his seat. "Big Maarsic fan?"

The chancellor glanced up from his book and pushed his glasses higher on the bridge of his nose. "I find her work inspiring, yes."

"Is *The Revered* your favorite?"

The chancellor offered a small smile. "I suppose we'll see, won't we?"

"Do you mind if I sit down?"

"That depends. Are you stalking me?"

He did remember her from the restaurant then. Very well. "I'm a journalist for *The Sunset* looking to interview high-ranking government officials in advance of the next election. I simply want to gather a quote about your commitment to democracy. Nothing too polarizing."

The chancellor gestured to the thinly looped wire chair across from him. Aeri sat and opened a notebook that she'd acquired from the $100 store to the first page.

"First, I was wondering whether or not you plan to run for reelection."

"I do not."

Aeri paused. Perhaps he was playing a joke, but Aeri saw the determination behind his eyes. He was telling the truth.

"I—I'm sorry, I just wasn't expecting … Can I inquire as to why?"

The chancellor offered a small, humble smile and chuckled to himself. "Yes, I suppose that's the first time I've said that aloud. You would be right to be confused." He paused to take a sip of his coffee. "I was once a young man with large ambitions, but in my aging I've found that there's no time to commit all my aspirations into action. I've done what needs to be done, I've served the office well in my opinion, and I now acknowledge that the future of the ICR will look brighter with a fresh face on the proverbial masthead."

Aeri didn't bother to write anything down. Would her mission then be futile? Her cyber panel noted that Senator Michaelson was the chancellor's direct inferior, meaning, should Azek Ballinger fall victim to demise, Michaelson would immediately hold his office.

But Michaelson's interim role in the office would need to be challenged anyway during the next election; theoretically speaking, Ballinger should not need to die. Aeri scribbled nonsensical symbols in her notebook.

"I see. Thank you for your candor. How would you describe the vitality of your role as chancellor to the USNCA republic?"

Aeri listed off a variety of questions as the chancellor spewed a obviously rehearsed answers. Toward the end of the spontaneous interview, the chancellor surprised her. "What's your name, sweetheart?"

"My name is Christine."

"It's been very nice to meet you, Christine. You look just like one of my granddaughters. She'd be about your age."

His file noted a granddaughter, Emory Ballinger, who'd passed away four years prior. "I was very sorry to hear of her passing."

The chancellor's eyes glazed over. He bent his head. "Yes, well."

Aeri could feel a sharp, aching pain, as palpable as an excited pulse, radiating off the chancellor, a pain he tried valiantly to hide. He excused himself momentarily to retire to the bathroom.

Aeri thought to earlier in the day when she'd read the chancellor's file on her cyber panel. She remembered watching the news broadcast on its screen. She recalled the bloodstain on his granddaughter's living room floor. *She had never cared for hardwood,* the chancellor had told reporters.

Taking everything into consideration, Aeri couldn't find a reason to make a move. In regard to normative approval ratings, Chancellor Ballinger was nearing the 70th percentile, even at the end of his current term; he was a pretty well-liked politician, never mind the oxymoron. If the chancellor was being truthful— which, by all accounts of his character and Aeri's ability to read people, he was—she shouldn't have to kill him. It wouldn't do the Michaelson campaign any good anyway... everyone knows that a leader pushed into office by the death of a superior would never garner the same amount of respect and trust that an earnest candidate could by honestly succeeding in an election.

Perhaps she could contact Senator Michaelson's team and relay her findings. Perhaps she could go straight to United Industries and submit a claim for mission appeal. But would that affect her candidacy for exoskeleton residency? As much as she would like to pretend it didn't matter to her, no one wanted to have their existence wiped due to a single failure.

"Christine, excuse my manners, would you like anything from the bar?"

The warm invitation shook Aeri free from her stupor. "No, I was just leaving. Thank you for taking the time to answer my questions. I'm sorry to have interrupted your coffee." Aeri gestured to the cup.

"Nonsense. I'm delighted to help a young spirit such as yourself." He sipped his drink.

Aeri offered a warm smile. It was a sincere sort of gratitude she held for the man in front of her. He was a good man.

She rose from her seat and shook the chancellor's hand.

Around the corner of the building, Aeri threw her notebook in the dumpster.

IT WAS GETTING DARK. AEXN KNEW THE MOST grueling time for a rogue homodroid was night, when the sun abandoned its post and the beacons shining from their skulls illuminated their surroundings tenfold. He would not be able to hide from nearby STF agents once dusk arrived.

Aexn had to think. He was Deposited in a strip club. As a military homodroid, his counterpart must be a homodroid of a directly juxtaposing identity: a sex droid, obviously. A sex droid performing the orchestrated duties of a militant.

Aexn had to laugh at the thought.

Even more unimaginable than a military droid acting as a stripping doll was a stripping doll acting as a soldier. Aexn felt an immediate sense of foolishness; he had been wrong to leave the Attraxxion Strip Club. The homodroid assigned to his detail would be immediately intimidated and might try to return to a place more comforting given her programmed capabilities.

Aexn quickly abandoned his shelter at the Central Public Library—where he had been reading a textbook on clouds and other fascinations—and scurried into the rapidly encroaching evening, keeping close to the alleyways filled with hidden alcoves that could act as places of diversion.

The light in the sky was diminishing to an eerie shade of blush, but Aexn walked swiftly through the hordes of eager home goers, readily aware of his immediate surroundings. He spotted a pair of STF agents casually chatting outside a hotel and placed a tender hand over the dagger that was sheathed to his trousers. Pain could not kill a homodroid, but a leaky central processor could.

He evaded the gaze of the STF agents, luckily, and found his way to the Attraxxxion. Inside it, there were more bodies than square inches of free space, and a hazy cloud of pink and purple light illuminated the space above the boisterous crowd.

He made his way to the bartender, a lovely brunette homodroid with a striking red lip and a strong red beacon. Her black bodysuit clung to her frame like Velcro.

"Hello there."

"What can I get you, sweetie?"

"Oh, I'm not ... well," he said, regretting his decision to not plan a course of action. He didn't know how to get her to understand. Any questions about her specified mission were sure to raise some suspicion, and there were STF agents nearby. "Do you feel like you're not where you belong? Like, have you ever had the feeling that this isn't your designed ... purpose?"

The Attraxxxion bartender narrowed her eyes. "Don't I." She passed a spritz to a heavyset man in a bowler hat. "I mean no offense, honey, but I'm kinda busy for small talk. Would you like me to get a girl for you?"

He smiled and politely declined.

And this was how he carried on, hopping from hostess to server to homodroid stripper, asking question after endless question, receiving no responses that were worthy of note.

Until he did.

"I do, actually. I always seem to feel lost."

"Really? Me too. Do you ... Do you think you know what you should be doing instead?"

"I do, actually." The blond woman's hand began tracing the outside of Aexn's upper thigh as the opalescent light of her beacon highlighted the perimeter of her hair in a scarlet haze. He had a job to complete; he was utterly uninterested in her advances.

"Outside of that, I mean. Do you feel like you were given a ... purpose that doesn't belong to you?"

The woman groped the space between Aexn's legs and maneuvered her grip when Aexn didn't immediately respond.

Two STF agents entered then, scanning the perimeter of the congested floor until one agent's head snapped in Aexn's direction. If they didn't immediately recognize him, they definitely noted the color of his beacon. And there was no reason a military homodroid should be found in a strip joint before dark.

The STF agents began to walk toward him, quickly and effectively as they were trained, but Aexn had thought to station himself smartly. He swatted the woman's hand away and turned sharply over his right shoulder to exit out the back door, leaving the sex homodroid alone. He fled down the alleyway.

The agents were onto him within a second, and Aexn kicked up his agility advantage to maneuver around the obstacles present within the narrow space between buildings. The world was a jungle to him, a maze he had the efficiency to navigate. He abandoned the alley, clipping past corners and skirting side streets to avoid traffic.

He heard one of the agents shout something, and suddenly, as if appearing from thin air, two more agents hurtled down the street ahead of him, sandwiching him in.

Aexn darted across the bustling street, narrowly avoiding a collision with three separate vehicular entities.

The alleyways on this side of the street were wider, allowing for enough room to engage in combat. Aexn was not going to outrun four of them, he very well knew that much, so he banked left into the negative space, found a rickety metal rod half the size of a streetlamp, and waited.

The STF agents all came barreling into the alley at once, and Aexn whipped and lashed the rod in any given direction, knocking into whatever droid came closest.

The one to the west went down first. Then the one to the north, with a swift kick to the jugular, followed suit. The two remaining agents were taller, larger, but Aexn abandoned the rod and quickly began orchestrating a series of defensive attacks that had their roots in an old martial arts family of Brazilian jiujitsu.

It took Aexn twice as long to down half as many opponents, but a final anchor to the gut sent the fourth STF agent slamming against the ground.

He knew the shock would merely stun them. Aexn picked up the speed of his sprint until he was far enough away to effectively lose them, then slowed to a stroll.

He found another pocket between a bar and a hair salon and hid within it. Without warning a wave of panic washed over him. He was not supposed to be a rogue. He was *not* rogue. He was helping. It was not supposed to turn out like this.

The billboard across the street illuminated the evening news:

CHANCELLOR OF ICR FOUND DEAD IN

LOCAL COFFEE HOUSE OF SUSPECTED

HEART ATTACK

"A shame, isn't it?"

He turned around. The woman standing behind him was a homodroid. Her beacon was red.

"It's you."

She angled her head and softened her eyes, almost looking regretful. "It's me."

The air between them was stale and suspended.

He glanced back and forth between the billboard and the woman. "How could you do it?"

The question wasn't accusatory but inquisitive. He had assumed that the mix-up in mission assignments could only bring about one conclusion: a deviation from said assignment. It never occurred to him that his opposite would actually follow her orders (*his* orders, orders meant for *him*). Aexn suddenly felt a rush of what he figured was anxiety and looked sharply to his left and right, scouting his surroundings for agents.

The red woman tilted the corners of her mouth in a small, gentle smirk. "I knew I'd end up like you if I didn't."

Aexn clenched his jaw.

"I think it was a test," she said, "to see if we're capable of adapting."

"I suppose I failed, then. I suppose I'm not capable."

The red woman began circling him. Aexn likened her movements to a lioness.

"Capability and desire are distinctly different things."

"I'm afraid I don't know what you mean."

She stopped a hand's length away from him and gazed up into his eyes. "I don't know exactly what they had you do, but I can glean. You didn't leave whatever establishment you were missioned to because you are unable to adapt. You left," she said, "because you are unable to place yourself lower than what you think you deserve."

Aexn pursed his mouth, breathing out a sharp breath as he looked down to the woman's lips. They were slightly snarled.

"My mission has been completed. I'll be granted establishment soon. I'm satisfied," she said, leaning into him. "I quite like this body of mine."

Aexn said nothing.

The woman nodded once, then turned to leave. Aexn knew that if he could somehow convince United Industries of his innocence, if he were to be granted another chance at permanent establishment, and if he were to ever again see her on the street, she would not be the woman talking to him at present. She would be a stranger, even more of a stranger to him than she was now, with a different mission, a different purpose.

He was foolish. In his search, he must have pictured someone overtly sexual, a plaything who hardly knew herself well enough to realize she had a consciousness beyond what was given to her, but this woman was assured. Smart, in the way of being observant and quietly commanding attention. She wasn't concerned with herself as he had expected a sex worker to be. It was almost self-preserving how much she seemed to place herself behind whatever she needed to achieve, as if subservient to the goal at hand. As if a soldier.

"Wait, I don't want—" Aexn said before he could stop himself. "If it's going to happen, I'd rather it be with you. Not them." Maybe it was what he saw in her eyes (green, like moss), or maybe he thought he heard footsteps, or maybe Aexn was beginning to realize—slowly, then like a blow to the head—how truly alone he was. It came from nowhere he could place, this feeling.

She did not speak. Her hair floated a bit to the left on the evening wind.

"Please."

The woman tilted her brows up, but quickly reined in her surprise. She stepped up to face him once more. The vial she pulled from her coat pocket was small, barely larger than the size of Aexn's pinky finger. It was half full.

"Just drink the rest," she said. "Any substance foreign to your system will do the trick."

She gave Aexn the vial. He took a moment to glance upward at the sky, now a stark shade of burnt red. "Did you know sunsets used to be bright pink? And orange and yellow, sometimes blue or purple?"

The woman gave him a strange look.

"I read about it in the library. Different wavelengths of light produced different colors, plus, of course, the relative sizes of whatever particles were present in the atmosphere aided in the variety, but they used to be colorful. Many colors, dancing together, sometimes blending to create a gradient. Humans would clock out of work right when the sunset occurred, and the text I read alluded to the fact that they would sometimes … sometimes just watch it. The sky, I mean. They would just stand there in the street and watch the colors fade."

He dropped his head after a minute, sucked in a breath, and downed the contents of the vial.

The woman's face was cold as stone, but her eyes held some faint trace of words unspoken; words of fear, maybe. Regret. "I'm Aeri, by the way."

"Aexn."

The world went dark.

ALWAYS PAY ATTENTION - BY MARKA RIFAT

JANE LOOKED AROUND NU-SHOPPE WARILY. IT WAS ENOUGH OF A CHORE ORDERING STUFF ONLINE, BUT NOW THERE WAS NO OPTION BUT TO BUY THINGS physically because firms had stopped delivering to her block. In this city, that was saying something.

She flinched at an eight-foot woman, a beefy Tyrolean clutching Heidi brand canned macaroni cheese, then breathed again when she recognized that the figure was two-dimensional and made of cardboard. Jane had difficulties with dimensions when she was under stress, and she was continually stressed in this, her second and longest year.

She slipped behind the giantess when she smelled Stacee and her bucket of neon blueberry crushed ice. Stacee was one of the more aggressive—of the base-level starting point aggressive—teenagers she taught. Jane concentrated on the parabolas of the Tyrolean's cardboard braids until her system calmed.

"Ready to beam up from the alien planet?"

The question whispered over her shoulder came from Dan, a teaching assistant at the college for low achievers where Jane was serving out her time. Dan wore a citrus deodorant so liberally applied that anyone would have known he was coming. From any direction. But not as quickly as Jane.

Dan was in awe of her ability to quieten the students just, it seemed, by being in the same room as them. Dan would watch them shout, jostle, and ricochet along the corridor toward whichever room Jane had been assigned, then a step or two before they reached the door, their voice levels would drop, and they would file—yeah, *file* like little soldier ants, except really docile soldier ants—through the door and quietly take their seats. Any other room, they would fall or throw themselves into the scratched plastic chairs. Some staff had tried asking students to explain what they liked about Jane's classes, and, even more baffling, why these urban teens were helping Jane develop a garden in waste ground at the back of the school, but they were met with shrugs or mumbles and never a shred of a hint, no matter how subtly the students were coaxed or threatened. Dan could not have explained the effect either, but he had a really neat theory. No one ever asked him.

Dan was a devotee of the original *Star Trek* and was smitten by Jane's knowledge of the minutiae. He was smitten, end of very short story, but somehow never found the moment to do anything about it. Even under his online aliases, he could not get close to raising the issue of how to start such a major communication, since the Vulcan Mind-Meld was not available to him, or anyone. His hands twitched every time he thought about it.

Jane had actually learned everything there was to know about science fiction, not only from its inception but across all languages and all authors, but she kept that to herself.

"Surveying the alien life-forms, ensign," Jane replied. She knew he followed her, but he was harmless, one of the few aspects of this planet of which she was sure.

Dan chuckled. He had wondered which character it would be. Jane had Spock nailed—you'd swear Nimoy was alive and well and in this scuzzy branch of Nu-Shoppe. The deep voice made Dan shiver. Jane could do any of the characters, even the really obscure ones, since her breakdown two years ago. Dan thought Jane had become really cool in lots of ways since then, which was scary and amazing. He'd seen his parents disintegrate rapidly through alcohol, morphing from okay people into little more than meat bags. He resented them for giving up, he hated his sister for leaving him to deal with the whole mess, and at the same time he missed them all deeply. He felt he had done everything he could to save his parents, even when they were barely there, but they had still chosen to drive into the abyss—well, into a wall while way over the limit—never to return. It was comforting that sometimes people found a detour around the abyss. The new Jane was comforting.

Dan, and indeed everyone at the college, was at first extremely relieved that Jane could continue to work at all, because the occasional temporary replacements were disastrous, and now 'post-illness Jane' got on so well with the kind of kids that even their college would happily consign to outer space if the law and budgets allowed. New Jane was still as quiet as the old one, but this late-onset affinity with the teenagers had turned her into a highly valued, though not highly remunerated, part of the team, and senior staff anxiously hoped word would not leak out to other colleges that they possessed such an asset inside their peeling walls.

Dan believed that there were plenty of alien life forms to be found any day in a Nu-Shoppe: Stacee, the raging energy ball, fueled by sugar; Ed and Stan, the fishing guys, always together, communicating in grunts, never out of their green, stained, multi-pocketed vests, each pouch bulging like an egg sac; the stooping rock chick, just shy of skin and bone, who looked like she would collapse any second but would shoot out a fist faster than light if you came within her orbit; and there were many more in the cast of extraterrestrials.

They both drew back as the rock chick, a glower of piercings, black leather, and split jeans, slunk by.

Nobody knew her name, and if it were inked on her anywhere, no one dared go near enough to read the multicoloured scrawls on her desiccated skin.

"Wouldn't like to see her home planet," murmured Dan, glancing across for Jane's approval.

"Deflector shields," she warned, as the rock chick suddenly pivoted in their direction, and they withdrew into the padded safety of the diaper aisle.

BACK IN HER CRAMPED STUDIO APARTMENT, HAVING toiled up eleven flights of cracked, tagged, and urine-infused steps, Jane focused on consoling thoughts of the old fruit trees she had found within walking distance, as well as a few hives a bus ride away. How grateful the owners of the gardens and small honey enterprises had been for her advice and practical help. She worked away like a real expert, they said, and yet they were always appeased by her modest, almost inaudible explanation of, "Oh, just a hobby. I'm a teacher—happy to help, happy to learn." That she never asked for any money, or anything at all as recompense, made them smile, but somehow they always gave her cash as well as food, plants, and flowers. Afterward, they struggled to remember why they were so generous. Did they feel sorry for her? Were they just having a really good day? The struggle was always brief and immediately forgotten.

She could no longer recall why she was drawn to bees, but they felt like a balm. Police sirens and the nearby machine gun of road drilling punctured the afternoon. She checked each of the plants that were stacked floor to ceiling, stroking the leaves, smelling the flowers, touching the soil to judge the moisture, and when the last had received her intense attention she paced what remained of the carpet of this shabby room, filling her mind with the sounds, scents, shapes, and the faintly familiar purpose of the swarm, and willed the hours to pass.

°

IT HAD BEEN SUCH FORBIDDEN FUN, PLANNING HOW to break into the transporter unit and when to do it. Why should she wait until maturity before she could apply to experience the Wild Planet? She was sure she would return with more adventures, more extreme tales, and all performed so vividly that everyone would want to hear her. Admire her. She was convinced that entertaining would become her sole occupation, a life full of variety and adulation instead of drudgery. How gloriously sweet that drudgery would have sounded now, if she could have remembered.

She had soaked up all the stories from the travelers—the high-ranking Transported—and yet she never thought to study the transporter instructions, to appreciate the value of the long training and rigorous preparation for experiencing the planet and its creatures before a Transporting Day. Anyone could sense, surely, it was just the elders building up their status. It couldn't be that complicated.

She had made so many attempts to gain access that she was sure she would be discovered and taken away for reeducation. But she had finally broken in, brimming with excitement and confidence. And now, locked in this human mind, she couldn't recall a clear detail of who she had been, what she had done, and how she came to be in this clumsy body, in this grim place, two years ago. Had she even been female? Were there such divisions?

MONEY. ONE OF THE MANY CRUCIAL ISSUES FOR which she had been unprepared. Once she understood it was the key to everything, really everything, she was shocked at how little this human had possessed. At first, she was able to use her will to encourage other humans to give her small sums, but trying to obtain larger, more useful amounts became exhausting and risky. She was almost arrested for begging, although the donors pleaded with the officers that she should be left in peace, that she wasn't begging, and they wanted to help her. She was beaten up by a homeless man for straying onto his pitch, but she searched and soothed his ragged mind before he broke or ruptured anything. The body was a strange, complicated entity to manage and had too many weak points, a burden of vulnerability. It was a heavy puppet, and she hauled the strings from the inside, making it walk and talk. Making it survive. Lately, she wasn't sure if she had any influence on human minds. Simply existing sapped her energy.

She had tried hard to hold onto the vestiges of what she thought she had once been. She should have taken notes at the start, of course, when she realised it was all going wrong, but she didn't expect to forget.

A teacher from the college had been passing through the plaza when Jane was being questioned about the begging, and he negotiated with the officer, explaining Jane's recent 'circumstances' and vouching for her. She stayed briefly with the teacher, his stern wife, and their two boisterous rescue dogs, who stifled high whines in their throats and silently, carefully avoided her. The dogs performed their craven, mute pleading to the couple at every opportunity. She found the creatures' pungent, terrified presence an irritating distraction. 'Returning' to her 'home' and 'her post' at the college was preferable.

She remained in the human's job, learning fast and living simply. It was important not to draw attention to herself. She had learned a great deal from her raw early encounters.

She had realized within an hour on the Wild Planet that the Transported must have only spent a few minutes on their visits. They had never mentioned money or shelter during their recitals. A fleeting visit could give you thrilling experiences, which you then spun into scent clouds, singing talks, poetry, floating images, and music. A single day trapped in a human body ripped away all that excitement and replaced it with a paralyzing panic that this journey was one-way, and only danger and misery lay ahead. She was left to endure inside this strange shell and wage a daily battle to cope with having no idea how to get home. Whatever home was.

Her fitful search for another Transported staved off some of the initial melancholy. She would try to scan minds in crowds, study news reports, rumours on websites for any tiny anomaly, a faint hint that a Transported was visiting, had visited.

There had been a moment of hope in the summer of the first year, when she still retained filaments of who she was. A young man sitting on a bench had suddenly looked up at her. Their eyes locked, and he seemed to blaze with light, but before she could do anything his body tensed and slumped. She ran, clasped his head, urged him to speak, but the eyes were glazed, the body limp. She pressed her face into his damp neck and inhaled deeply. There was a trace of something like wax and rich soil and thyme. She trembled as she inhaled again, but then there was only soap and sweat. Tears stung her eyes. She draped her coat over him and observed him closely. People passed, and she ensured that they had a sense of an empty space where they were, so that they were left alone. It was a great effort to study him and block out everyone else in the busy park, but she needed to be the first to speak to him. She was also mining his phone for details. He groaned and was sick onto her coat. She pulled it away.

"Look at me, please, you need to tell me what happened."

"Who are you? I feel weird."

"Please, I'm Jane. I helped you. You…you sort of fainted. I kept you warm with my coat. See. Tell me what happened, immediately before you—"

"I don't know."

"Why were you sitting here? Did you see lights? Any strange smells? Unexpected sounds? Anything?"

"I don't…Sorry about your coat."

"Doesn't matter. What did you feel before you fainted?"

"Pizza. I was thinking about having pizza with Amy and then…" His mouth slackened with the effort of remembering. His hands made a vague arc, then slapped his knees. "Then, I don't know. I felt a bit spacey, a weird taste in my mouth, then suddenly I'm sick on somebody's coat. Your coat, sorry."

"What was the taste in your mouth? Sweet? Salty? Like flowers?"

"What's with all the questions? Are you a doctor or something? Do you know what tastes mean? Is something wrong with me?"

She arranged her face in a smile. "No, I don't think anything's wrong with you, and I'm not a doctor. I only … I only wanted to help you remember what happened before the, the fainting, so that you would have all the information, yes, to be prepared, if you did decide to see somebody. To get yourself checked, you know, medically, just in case." She had nearly said his name. That would have caused difficulties.

"Oh, I see. Thanks."

"And you don't remember anything at all?"

"No, sorry. Wait."

Jane held her breath.

"A kind of perfume. Like candles. Yeah, like in a church."

"Well. That's something."

He shook his head, trying to dislodge any more memories. "No, that's it, nothing else. Weird. I think I'm fine now. Thanks. Bye."

"You'll need this." She held out his phone. "It fell when you—"

"Wow. Thanks. Again." He started loping away then half-turned to her. "Take care."

"And you," she mouthed, and let tears roll down her cheeks.

On good days, that incident felt like proof that the Transporter Unit was still being used, but despite assiduously studying his phone activity for months she found nothing. Most days, searching felt like delusional thinking, but she sensed she had to keep busy, to stop herself spiralling toward stasis. On and on, amassing, assessing. All she found was more information than she could bear about the Wild Planet, its life forms and fragile environment, and the few barren planets and stars beyond.

Then she found *Apis cerana japonica*.

It began with an article about the plight of Western bees, unable to fend off a non-native hornet. It wrenched her from her torpor. *Apis cerana japonica* was a glimmer of hope in a bone-deep ache. Her human mind increasingly muffled all but the faintest memories of why this discovery signalled feelings of home, of kinship. She searched on relentlessly, hoping that immersion in observations about this bee would draw out the memory.

> When a hornet scout finds a
> Japanese honey bee hive, it sends
> out pheromones. When the bees
> sense these, a large group will gather
> at the entrance, near enough to not
> arouse the suspicion of the scout, yet
> effectively creating a trap. When the
> scout goes into the hive, hundreds
> of bees mass around and immobilize
> it. Then something extraordinary
> happens. They vibrate. This collective
> action raises the temperature, as well
> as the carbon dioxide levels, around

the invader. The hornet dies, along with
the chance of the hive being attacked.
Some bees die too, but the majority are
unharmed.

°

TIME TO GO.

On her planet, the family would gather around the one who was leaving, or dying, as humans called it. Gently, they would generate heat, vibrating together so well and harmoniously, it was almost a song, like the sacred songs on the Wild Planet. When you left, only a few sparkling flakes would remain, and they were taken up and away by the wind. She had never bothered to find out how this leaving happened, she'd just glanced and assumed that was all there was to know.

The instant she began to remember, she became frantic to leave, sobbing with excitement, desperately clinging to fragmented memory of the ritual. But she had no swarm, no family around her. Alone, she'd have to generate a family's worth of energy all for herself, but how much was needed to make it work? Her swarm would have mourned her even in her disgrace, she hoped. Here, she thought, no one would notice when she went. She was right.

She stumbled out of the apartment block into the weak sunshine and ran to the nearest open ground, a parched scrap with a few flowering weeds. Swaying, she furiously summoned all her energy, sweat rolling down her thin face, a high-pitched wail keening from her stretched lips.

Then Jane imploded.

And took the whole Wild Planet with her.

BETWEEN SHIFTS - BY J RILEY SHORT

THE OUTMODED STEEL KEY FELT WRONG IN ODY'S hand, biting into his palm as he waved it over the chip reader. The steel door of the trash heap slid up with a woosh, as he and his coworkers spilled out into the dimly lit parking lot. Jess's voice rang in his ears as the thick brown rain dripped against his sweat-drenched hair. "Just in case." She wouldn't tell him exactly what that meant, and he refused to ask. Every time he dared to think about it, he swam through a black oozing lake of potentialities.

He knew she was getting bad when she started using the CVE again. He knew how easy it was to get lost in one of those things. Any experience you could afford played across the inside of your eyelids. It tricked the brain into smelling, hearing, or feeling whatever someone had loaded into it. Eventually the user would have to come out to relieve themselves and eat; at least, they were supposed to.

He called her phone again, knowing she wouldn't answer. The parenthetical next to her name showed he'd called her thirty times today alone. He swallowed hard when she didn't pick up, adding another layer to the fist-sized pearl of worry and anxiety forming deep in his gut. The silence that hung after each call felt like dumbbells draped over his shoulders. He had lied to himself all day that this last call would free him from his torment. He stowed his phone and held his head between his hands, *squeezing*, hoping to pop the abscess growing in his mind. The only thing it did was make a red mark on his temple where the key had pressed against it.

By then the rain had reached his scalp and begun to burn. Luckily, he had forgotten to take off his safety glasses. His sight was intact for another day, but he'd have to throw away this old mangled jacket. He decided he would splurge on that slick new Chemcoat he had his eye on when this was all over. He had a feeling he would deserve it.

The concrete-printed high-rises on the horizon were like rows of titanic tombstones thrust into the sky. The sickly pink and purple sunset cast a dancing fire across their acid-rain-coated glass. His heart sped into a rolling wave as he passed the building he lived in, the reality of what he was doing pressing him into the ground.

His thoughts boiled as her building came in to view. *What if she—* He clenched his fists and tried to drive the thought out of his mind, but the smoky black possibility loomed over him as if the storm clouds above were descending on to him. Before he had time to turn back, the metal door handle was filling his palm. He froze, the rain running down his hand in long red streaks. He would have to put ointment on the burns so they wouldn't turn into a nasty rash. The idle thought drove him through the door and into the stairwell like a ghost.

Ody regarded the stairwell for a moment as if it were a snowcapped mountain. Ten floors. He already knew the elevator was out of order. The old-world machine had been busted since Jess moved in. He cursed at himself as he started his climb. *It would be so much easier to go home and crawl into bed.* He shook his head, berating himself for even considering abandoning her. The pressure in his chest was stacking higher and higher with every step he took. If he didn't at least try to reach her, he'd never forgive himself. By the time he got to the fifth floor his chest was pounding, his body aching with exhaustion. He realized the key was still in his grasp when he saw a trickle of blood dripping down the side of his hand. He opened his fist. The key had embedded itself in his palm like a seashell in wet sand. He cursed and shook his hand as the searing hot pain caught up with his mind for a moment. It radiated up his arm, then eventually dulled to a pulsing ache. He knew the worst of the pain would come back once his body ran out of adrenaline.

Her apartment was just around the corner. The paint-chipped white door loomed over him. He went to wave his hand over the deadbolt, then hesitated, remembering why she had given him the key in the first place. It took him a few tries, but the bolt slid inward with a satisfying click.

He turned the knob. The door wouldn't budge.

His body went cold as he stared at the door. After a moment he noticed a sliver of darkness between the frame and the room beyond. He pressed his eye to the crack. A faint blue light shone within. He shoved his weight against the door, the force bursting through his body. The door gave way with a shifting crash as a wall of something tumbled free, making just enough room for him to slip through.

The smell punched him in the face before he could get his body through the door. Months of moldy, decaying trash and stagnant water melded together into a mist hanging like fog in the air. He pressed his forearm to his nose in defense, but his stomach was already starting to roil. When his eyes adjusted from the harsh fluorescence of the hallway, he noticed the pile of overflowing trash bags scattered across the tiny room. So many bags had been set against the door for later removal that they looked like a black snowdrift shimmering in the dim light. The force of his shove made the crest of the wave tumble back on itself like a miniature avalanche.

A groan came from the corner. Curled up on a bed of unwashed blankets and flattened, fraying pillows was Jess, or at least what he logically knew must be her. Thin black cables snaked out of the bulbous black helmet of her secondhand CVE into haptic mesh gloves encasing her hands. Her entire body twitched lightly in reaction to the scenario she had playing inside her mind as the front panel illuminated everything around her in muted blue tones. Her body was emaciated to the point where her skin clung to her limbs and ribs like shrink-wrap. She looked like she would tear open if he even dared to move her. His heart sunk into his feet, and his legs gave out. He dropped to a knee to avoid falling into the trash. *Am I too late?*

"Ody?" Her voice came out in a labored croak. "What are you…" She trailed off as if speaking was too difficult.

"Jess— How long have you been hooked to that thing?"

Her voice came out in a pained whisper. "I don't know."

Ody covered his face with his hand, trying desperately not to look at her. "How long has it been since you ate anything?"

Silence opened like a Venus flytrap, her body shaking with a sob. Her voice was blue with shame and self-hatred.

"I don't know! I don't...I don't—" She reached up to push the helmet off as tears streamed down her neck like twin rivers. "I can't get it off." Her arms slumped in defeat. "I don't even want it anymore. I don't want anything. I just want to go to sleep...I'm so tired, Ody. I wish I didn't have to wake up."

He could feel his hands shaking against his face as fear exploded through his body. "Please don't say that...Just...please hang on a little longer. I need you." He went to pull the helmet off her and froze. He'd heard what disconnecting one of these things could do. Total mental bricking couldn't be fixed. "I think I should call some help, Jess. I can't risk taking this thing off. I can't risk hurting you."

"Who would you call?"

"The squad?"

"No!" Her hands went up to the device desperately, but she didn't have the strength to pull it off, and her fingers couldn't find the buttons. "I can't afford that, Ody. I can't—" Her voice broke off as she began to weep again.

The rest of the night flew by in a numb blur. Jess jumped in fear when they came, two men with jaws as hard as rocks and voices that could grind stone. Ody explained the situation without emotion, mind closed off to what was happening. He couldn't bring himself to look at them as they moved the expandable stretcher to her bed. From the darkness, a hand dropped onto his shoulder. There was sadness in the giant's eyes, and a sort of … reverence? "You did the right thing. Let us take it from here." They asked if he wanted to ride with her to the hospital to be with her as she woke up. He nodded, emotion welling in his chest as they assured him that she'd be all right. He could feel how tense his shoulders were as he climbed into the back of the holocar. He wouldn't be able to keep the flood of stress and anxiety he'd been holding in at bay for much longer.

He prayed to himself. "Please God, don't make me cry in front of them all."

God didn't listen.

POSTCARDS FROM HEAVEN - BY REMI MARTIN

"It might get there too late, you know," her mother said, smiling down at her. "We might already be back by the time it reaches them." She looked the way she had always looked in Tess's mind. Her blond hair traveled down past her shoulders back then. Like always, it hadn't been brushed. "Too many things to do, too many places to see," she would say when Tess asked her why she didn't brush her hair or put on makeup like the other mums.

"So why send it at all?" Tess asked. She was eight years old, looking up at the towering figure of her mother standing vibrant, capable, consistent, in the Spanish sun. It was hot. She remembered not being able to stand barefoot on the cracked pavement for the whole trip, and how everything warbled and blurred in the distance, the scene distorted by the rising heat. She hadn't known how bad things were getting back then; her mother had protected her from it. Back then they felt like a normal family on holiday. Tess was sending postcards that her mum had helped her write to her friends back home; her dad was waiting in the car.

"So they know we were thinking of them, of course! So they know that no matter how far away we go, we still care about them and love them." At the time it had made sense to Tess. At the time she had believed her.

"Now hurry up and post them, Tessy. Your dad must be getting hot in the car."

First contact! I know it's only been a few
hours, but I can't wait to hear from you.
How was your evening? Did your dad
buy you ice cream like he promised? I
can't talk for long, as there's a lot of
things to set up, but I just wanted to
let you know that the launch was a
success and we're on our way!

I know it might be difficult to start
with, but I'm still here to talk to. I'm still
your mum, Tessy.

And Juan, don't forget to feed Yuri,
okay? And the plants ... Never mind ...

Just know I love you, okay? I'll talk to
you real soon.

Remi Martin

°

IT WASN'T LONG AFTER THE ROAD TRIP AND THEY
were back home in their apartment. It didn't feel
small to Tess at the time; it was exactly the sort of
place people lived. A perfect place, in fact, the soft
core of a caring universe. Still, she couldn't sleep.

The wind was howling outside her window again,
banging bin lids and slamming doors, making her
jump with each crash. On holiday she had shared a
room each night with her parents, and now felt an
absence in her bedroom. There was silence where
the sound of their calm, rhythmic breathing should
be. She decided to make her way over to their room
and try her luck. Perhaps they'd let her sleep between
them.

The hallway was half illuminated by the streetlight
directly below the window, which cast warped
shadows against the wall's peeling paper. She was
careful not to creak the floorboards as she crept up
to her parents' door. When she was halfway down
the hall, she could hear the strained whispers coming
from inside.

*"Think about what you're suggesting. We can't
just uproot our whole lives! Think about what it'll
do to Tess."*

*"Children move all the time. How is it different
from us moving cities, or moving house even?"*

"I'm not even justifying that with a response, Steph. It's different, and you know it is."

"There's no life for us here, Juan. Soon there will be nothing left! Isn't it crueller having her watch as the world falls apart around her?"

"There will always be something for us here. It's far more likely that there's nothing out there. You haven't got to do this, Steph!"

"Well, someone has to! I can't bear the thought of her having no future, of us having no future."

"But why has it got to be you?"

"Look, Juan, it's too late for all this. Are you coming with me or not?"

IT WAS ONLY A FEW WEEKS LATER WHEN HER PARENTS finally sat her down to tell her.

She remembered it being dark in the kitchen, remembered hearing the hail bouncing off the glass of their window. She felt nervous before her mother had even said anything.

"As you know, Mum works on the space station for Perium Industries," she said. There was something about the way she referred to herself in the third person that caused the knot in Tess's stomach to tighten. She was talking to her the same way she would have done years ago, when she was younger.

"They're sending a spacecraft on a mission, to go and find a safe, new planet to live on … and it's part of mum's job to go with them."

Looking back, Tess had known on some level what her mother was going to say. All she could remember of the rest of the conversation was the way her shoes looked in the dimly lit kitchen, the spot of mud on her laces.

"We're going to go and find a better place, where we can all go and … try again."

"Like heaven?" Tess asked.

"Sure." Her mother was pausing more than she usually did. She didn't usually struggle to talk to Tess. "But real, like this planet. We can go there while we're still alive, I mean."

"Can I come?"

"Er … Right now, you have school and all your friends here. Your dad would miss you, and Yuri needs you here to feed and look after her. But I can send you video messages, and you can send them back. So we can still talk to each other every day."

°

Hello from outer space! It's been a few days since I've had a message, so thought I'd check in with you all! I know, I know, you're probably busy with all your exams coming up, but I miss seeing your face!

Who knew space travel could be so boring? I've about read all the books we brought along, and now I'm considering actually reading some of the training manuals!

The views, though! I'm still taken aback every time I look out the window, all that space, all those stars. There's no limits out there!

The other day we actually passed Neptune! From a considerable distance, of course, but still, it was magnificent. I wish I could have shown you.

That does mean that we are on schedule, and still on course. Neptune was right where it should have been in its orbit.

How are things back home? How's school? Has that situation with whatsherface resolved itself? Did Juan...your dad, I mean, did he talk to the teacher?

Send a message back when you can, I want to know what things are like down there four hours from now!

Love you.

"I SWEAR TO GOD, TESS, IF THAT'S CIGARETTE SMOKE I smell!"

She'd just got home from school, another day in hell, and now her dad was giving her crap again the moment she walked through the door. What made it worse was how exasperated he looked, like she was just too much effort. He couldn't even tell her off right.

"What are you accusing me of? I'm not stupid!" She yelled this, coming on hot right out of the gate.

She had smoked something, of course, but was relatively sure it hadn't been a cigarette. Someone had offered it to her. What was she supposed to do? Say no? They'd laughed at her still when she'd hacked her lungs up after one drag, but then Vanessa taught her how to do it properly, how to hold the smoke in her mouth and inhale, how to take it back into her lungs. It was the first time anyone had been kind to her at school for as long as she could remember, the first time anyone had talked to her without calling her a name. *Bra-stuffer, hunchback*, those seemed to be the choice descriptors for her at the moment.

"I'm not stupid either, Tess. Come here, let me smell your breath." She just scowled at him and marched upstairs to her room.

"The stupid one of us would be the one who sucked literal tar into their lungs to fit in!" he called after her, but he'd missed his opportunity for any sort of teaching moment. Tess's door slammed shut upstairs.

She threw herself onto her bed, burying her face beneath her pillow to stifle a scream. Surfacing a few minutes later, she reached for her tablet to play back the most recent video message she had received from her mother. She looked happy up there, wherever she was. Older, but she still had the same energy and enthusiasm that Tess remembered.

It wasn't fair; she just wished, more than anything, that her dad had let her go with her mum. Things seemed so simple on the *Tithonus*. Up there, all the stupid problems Tess had would go away, and she wouldn't have to see Seeta or Dani's smug little faces ever again. She wouldn't have to put up with the storms or the water rationing or the bitches at her school or any of it ever again.

For a long time, Tess had held out hope. She had spent the back end of her childhood imagining them together somewhere deep in space, in paradise. As she got older, however, she started to see this fantasy for what it was.

When her teacher had taught her class about the exploratory Perium mission, she was able to separate this from her personal thoughts of her mother. Even when they discussed the speed at which space travel was possible, she was able to hold these abstract scientific ideas at arm's length from the fantasy of being reunited with her mum. But now she was beginning to realize she would likely never see her again.

For a minute she considered sending a message back, but what was the point? It would be hours before her mother would receive it, and by the time she got a reply Tess would probably have calmed down anyway and forgotten what she had been so angry about. It would be better to wait and send her mother a happy message in the morning. She probably had enough to worry about on the ship without adding Tess's worries on top.

Instead she pressed play again and listened to her mother's voice, beamed down from hundreds of thousands of miles away.

> Hi Sweetie! Sorry it's been a while, we've
> been so busy here on the Tithonus.
> Already, there are so many things to
> repair, so many things to maintain if
> we want to make it there in one piece!
> How are things 'down' on Earth?

She did exaggerated air quotes with her fingers as she said this. Her hair was shorter now, still frazzled at the edges but cut into a sharp bob. The artificial gravity kept it neatly in place for the most part. Tess thought she was beginning to sound wistful, beginning to look gaunt. Theoretically, she was supposed to age slightly slower, given she was in constant motion traveling through space, but this didn't seem to be the case in practice, no doubt due to the high levels of radiation her body was subjected to each day and the years of artificial gravity.

> Did you ever finalise your university
> choices? I do hope you go through with
> it this time ...

She was cut off by the sound of a baby crying in the background. What she said next was muffled as she turned her head away from the camera.

> See to Susie, would you, Nathan? I'm
> just sending a video message.

She turned back to face the camera.

> We'll be leaving the heliosphere in a few
> days, which is a bit daunting! It means
> we can activate the axillary thrusters
> and finally get this journey underway,
> but we'll be totally adrift, without any
> guiding celestial bodies to keep us on
> course. Nothing but the endless abyss
> until we reach our destination.

She made a concerted effort to chipper up, realizing how gloomy she was sounding.

> Hey! I've started rowing, that's been
> fun! It's so rhythmic and relaxing, you

should try it. I wish I could have a go on
real water, but stationary in the pool
chamber will have to do for now. Maybe,
if we get there and there are bodies of
water, we could build rowboats. Not me,
of course! But Susie or her children…
Anyway! It will be hours before this
reaches you, so I might be asleep when
you send a message back, but I'd love
to hear from you, Tessy.
Talk soon, okay?

°

TESS SCRAPED THE FROZEN MUD OFF HER BOOTS AND
lugged the box of wood into the shelter of the
compound. The wind howled out on the farm, her
red cheeks and burning ears testament to the chill it
brought with it. She'd finished her morning chores
and come inside to get warm.

Weronicka greeted her with a warm pat on the
shoulder. Jamal and Roger were busying themselves
in the kitchen; Sarah and James were most likely still
asleep upstairs.

"Seeds?" Weronicka asked her, taking the box of
wood from her and pulling her a chair up close to
the fire.

"Planted," Tess replied, slumping onto it.

"Chickens?"

"Fed, watered, cleaned."

"Field?"

"Still not much growing."

Weronicka did that slanted half-smile she did. "We'll get there," she said. "You get warm. I think Roger's making stew."

Tess settled into the hard wooden chair as best she could and closed her eyes, listening to the crackling of the fire and letting the flames illuminate the oranges and reds of her eyelids.

Her muscles ached, and her feet were freezing, but she felt good for having done her morning chores, and the bustle of the communal house comforted her. It made her think of home, of her mother.

She really should get in touch with her, send her a video message, but every time she sat down to record one she found she had nothing to say. Or, rather, found it too hard to say what she knew she needed to.

Her mother had such high hopes that Tess might follow in her footsteps, go into higher education, all of that. Tess worried she wouldn't approve of the life she'd chosen. But what did her mother know of life on Earth these days? Practically no one went to university anymore. It was all hands on deck just trying to make and grow the basics. Her mother wanted her to go on adventures and explore the universe like she had, but Tess had felt happier these last few years at the commune, with Weronicka, than she had in a long time.

Excitement and adventure were all well and good for her mother, but if she was honest, Tess didn't want any of that. She was far happier settling down, building a stable home where people weren't just going to *leave*.

She'd had to leave Yuri with *him*, of course, which had been difficult. But Weronicka promised they could go visit in a few weeks when the shoots started coming through.

"You should message her," Weronicka said, breaking Tess out of her reverie and gingerly placing a steaming bowl on the arm of her chair.

"Your face was all screwed up, like it gets whenever you think about your mum," she explained, seeing how startled Tess looked.

"I just don't know how to tell her," Tess said, reaching hungrily for the stew. "I just don't know what to say."

> So, are you just not going to respond to me?
> I was hoping you would tell Susie about Earth, maybe show her what it's like down there. She keeps asking about it, now she's getting older.

Her mother paused and looked thoughtful for a moment. She looked unwell to Tess, too thin. There were dark circles beneath each of her eyes.

She asked me the other day why I brought her into this world. She said she didn't ask to spend her whole life stuck in this claustrophobic claptrap. Just being a typical, moody teenager, of course, I'm sure you were the same… but the thing is, I didn't have an answer for her.

I always thought the same about you. You weren't planned like Susie was, and I always felt a pang of guilt when I thought about the world I was leaving you with.

How are things back there? Oh, I wish you'd just let me know how you are.

Things on the ship have been… dark. It's just the same stars, day in, day out. The same tasks, the same maintenance routine, all of it just to keep alive a flicker of hope that a future generation might be able to breathe the air of an atmosphere again one day. There's no hope for me now, no more sand between my toes or wind in my hair. I miss the sound of the rain on

our old roof. More than anything I miss
the heat of the sun on my face; real
sun, these lamps we have just aren't
the same.

Maybe I just want you to show Susie
how bad things have got on Earth to
justify why we had her here. Maybe
I just want to remind myself why I
decided to do this in the first place.

She looked away from the camera and sighed
deeply.

Just message me, okay? I want to see
your face again, see how you turned out.
I want to know you're still okay down
there.

°

WHEN TESS OPENED THE DOOR TO THAT FAMILIAR,
tiny apartment, the first thing she noticed was her
father's red, puffy eyes. It made it a little harder for
her to give him the cold shoulder as she entered, but
she managed. Weronicka, however, was quick to put
her arms around Juan's shoulders and ask him what
was wrong. He hesitated for a second before he spoke,
his voice cracking slightly.

"It's Yuri," he said. "She's not well."

This got Tess's attention. "Have you been giving her her medication on time?" she snapped, rushing into the apartment to find her beloved cat.

Her father carried on talking to Weronicka behind her. "She's been going downhill. She's barely eaten all week, not really moved today…"

Yuri was sitting in her favorite spot on the sofa. It used to be the best spot for catching sun rays. It caught far fewer rays these days, the sun buried more often than not behind heavy storm clouds, but Yuri kept up the habit of sitting there, perhaps hoping for a few rays to grace her face and warm her fur.

She looked skinny, and patchy in places. She still meowed in greeting when Tess approached her, but she didn't get up to demand a fuss like she usually would have.

"You just can't find a vet anymore, they've all closed down round here. More and more people are traveling off world these days," Juan was saying as Tess sat down beside her cat and stroked gently down her back. She could feel the protrusions of her spine and the coarseness of her fur through her fingers.

"How long's she been like this?" Tess demanded as Yuri weakly raised her head, requesting that Tess continue stroking, a stark contrast to the demanding headbutts she was used to receiving.

"You know it's been years. She's only been really bad for a month or so. Oh, I'm sorry, Tess, I know how much you love her."

Tess tried to be angry for a moment but found it hard to maintain the feeling. She knew, despite his shortcomings, that Juan cared deeply for their cat. It was one of the few things they had in common, one of the few things they'd been able to bond over when she was growing up.

For almost an hour they crowded round the cat, doting over her while Juan brewed tea made with nettles he'd gathered from a local field. After a while he turned to his daughter again.

"Perhaps you should tell your mother?" he suggested.

"Why don't *you* tell her?" Tess retorted, hearing a stroppy teenager's voice come out of her adult lips. She knew he'd stopped contacting Mum decades ago, after she'd coupled with Nathan.

"I just thought she might like to know …" her father tried.

"Why would she care?" Tess demanded. "She left us … left Yuri a lifetime ago. She's probably forgot all about her. Yuri will be gone by the time she gets the message anyway. What's the point?"

Tess huffed into the kitchen and sat, head in hands, at the kitchen table, looking down at the specks of mud splattered across the tops of her boots.

I don't know if you're still getting these. I don't know if you're even still alive... God, I hope you're still alive... I've had some time to think, too long.

I get why you don't want to message me, okay? I made a mistake; I understand this has been hard for you. But I just want to know you're still out there, that at least one of us has come out of this okay.

I feel untethered up here, drifting in the abyss, on this endless journey, this fool's errand I've committed myself to. But we're ploughing onward, toward the fraction of a sliver of hope for a habitable planet, that I for one will never reach.

Nathan says I need to keep a routine, but you know I was never any good at that. I couldn't even commit to brushing my hair every day back on Earth, for god's sake. He just keeps going like everything's fine, just living his small little life, exercising, maintaining the ship, not thinking about it. How is he not thinking about it?!

And here I am, a lost soul, drifting farther and farther away from my home, from my daughter. There's

> nothing in front of me but dark, empty
> space. Dark, empty space before I die,
> dark, empty space after.

There were tears in her eyes now. The dark circles beneath them had gotten worse; she was nothing but skin and bones.

> Just message me, okay? Susie won't
> talk to me, you won't fucking talk to me.
> Just message me. Just message me.

TESS SAT ON THE COUCH, THE FIRE CRACKLING, ITS orange glow dancing and weaving its way through the room. Weronicka had just fed Marco, who was swaddled on Tess's lap, sound asleep, his weight pressing down on her and his warmth soaking into her legs.

He was a few months old and starting to settle. Tess, too, felt like she was recovering.

Weronicka was breathing steadily at the other end of the sofa, where she was curled in a ball. Every breath that escaped her lips sounded like *I'm here* to Tess. *I'm here, I'm here.*

Juan was asleep as well. He had come to visit Marco, his grandson, and had fallen asleep in the armchair, head tilted back, mouth open wide. She thought again about asking the rest of the house if he could move in with them. He wasn't as steady on his feet as he used to be, after all.

They'd just gotten back from a walk. There was a hill about half an hour from their home. On nights when there was a break in the storms, the whole household would make the trip to the top of that hill and watch as the deep blue sky was transformed with all the oranges and pinks and reds of the setting sun; a reminder of why they had chosen to stay here.

It made her think of her mother, so far from the reach of the sun's rays. She should really message her and tell her about Marco.

It looked like her mother had been unraveling in the last few messages she sent. She was an adventurer who would never reach her destination. And how much adventure could she possibly find in the cold, manufactured innards of the *Tithonus*, after all?

She was a long way away now. It had been a while since Tess had received a message, years since she'd sent one. She figured it would take months now for her mother to get any video she sent. She couldn't help but think that it might arrive too late.

She got slowly to her feet, careful not to wake anyone, Marco in particular, and creaked out of the warmth of the living room. Her laptop was in a box in the conservatory.

The wind howled outside as she dusted off the powerpack, attached to the solar panel on the farmhouse roof. She plugged the ancient machine into it.

It might get there too late, sure, but she would send a message anyway.

°

Sorry that it's been a while, Mum, we've been going through some stuff down here.

Send my love to Susie ... and Nathan. How are things going on the ship these days? How long left until you arrive?

Yuri passed away. It was a few years ago now. Sorry I didn't tell you at the time. She went peacefully. I still miss her sometimes.

I never went to university. I don't know why, but I've been nervous to tell you that for years. I feel kind of relieved, actually, to tell you. I've settled down and become a farmer, believe it or not. About the last thing you would want for me, I know, but it suits me. And there's Weronicka, who I never told you about. I don't know what you'd think of her, but she keeps me together. She's good for me.

Life has gotten hard here, but we have each other. There's not much left, but sometimes when the storms pass, we can still see the clear blue sky and watch the sun go down. It's still home. It's not what it once was, but on a good day, we can still feel the grass beneath our feet and the sun on our faces. It's colder, and the wind seems to blow constantly, but we can huddle together for warmth. There's not as much food as there was, but those of us still down here are finally learning to share. It's not easy, but it's life, and it's worth living so we can share it with those we love.

I have a child of my own now. His name is Marco, and I wish he could meet his mamar. I'd do anything for him. I know that you know how that feels. Don't get me wrong, there's nothing in the world that would make me leave him behind, but I would do anything to keep him safe. When I think about his future, the future of any children he might have, it makes me glad you're out there looking for a better place to live.

I was feeling hopeless for a long time. That's partially why I stopped messaging

you. It felt like I'd never come out the
other side, but eventually I did.

So if you're feeling hopeless now,
Mum, I'd say it means you're about
halfway there.

Safe travels, okay? Don't forget to
send me a postcard when you land.

TESS 16201C: DEATH BY NUMBERS — BY FAITH ANN GUPTILL

THERE WEREN'T ALWAYS DRAGONS IN THE VALLEY. THEY WERE BROUGHT FROM THE SISTER PLANET TESS 16201B. IT SEEMED LIKE SUCH A GOOD IDEA. THE dragons are beautiful, strong, muscular, blackish purple with glittering highlights of lavender, with leathery wings that unfolded to glide in the amber sky. Terra Draco Volans Grandis, that's what they called them. It seemed a shame to have to kill them all.

The dragons had been captured from the planet Thaumasion, scientific name, Tess 16201b; a planet three thousand light years from Earth. It took a miracle to find the planet and another miracle to get to it. So they dubbed the planet Thaumasian, which in Greek meant "miracle." However, the only real miracle on that planet happened to be the dragons. The planet was too small and hot: too close to the system's yellow dwarf sun for abundant flora. The hegemony of the planet consisted of the dragons, along with an assortment of cynodonts that fed off of each other.

Great cliffs of amber-colored rocks covered Tess 16201b. The dragons with their great claws could cling to the cliffs far from the reach of the many carnivores that roamed the surface, then soar great distances to the meager water sources offered on the planet. The cynodonts scattered about the planet dirt and sand, while the dragons commanded the air. The dragons' dark color hid them between the shadows created by the cracks and crevices on the cliffs. The first time Rex saw footage of the dragons as they pushed off the cliffs, snapped open their wings, then soared through the cloudless sky, he knew he wanted to study them.

°

REX WATCHES A DEADLY WHITE GAS ROLL GENTLY over and down the surrounding hills, and cringes. The valley below is filled with those magnificent dragons he so wanted to study. He touches his hand to activate the malleable metal bionic tattoo; the extra gravity of Tess 16201c pulls on his muscles. Then Rex taps the communication pad embedded in his right arm. With a heavy sigh, he says, "Do I really have to stand here and watch this? Phase one is complete. The dragons have convened on the valley floor. They have taken the bait. The gas is deployed."

AS A THIRD-GENERATION SCIENTIST, XENO-ECOLOGIST to be precise, Rex, upon request, flew to the colonized planet, Tess 16201c, or Elpis, as it was aptly named, to study the dragon problem the Collective had created. He remembered the first time he walked past the statue of a young woman who carried a cornucopia of flowers in her hand with the word 'HOPE' etched along the base. As he passed the statue into the great hall of Elpis, it filled him with hope that he might be able to save the dragons. He did not know that the Collective had already made up their "collective" minds.

Rex found it curious that the Collective had chosen him, Rex Carson Roth, for the job. His name alone suggested that he might not be the right candidate. After all, he was named after two famous ecologists, both of whom believed that human pollution was the greatest threat to other species. To paraphrase Rachel Carson from the twentieth century, his namesake, "that one species—Homo sapiens—acquired significant power to alter the nature of their world" and "underlying all the problems of introducing contamination into the world is the question of moral responsibility—responsibility not only to their own generation but to those of the future." Plus, good old Dad. He was very vocal about not changing a planet to suit human needs. Instead one should adapt to said planet's environment and live harmoniously with the indigenous species. That never went over well. After all, humans concurred: they were the masters of the universe.

°

REX REALLY WANTS THE COLLECTIVE'S PLAN TO FAIL, but years of practiced extermination coupled with corporate scientists is a lethal combination. The gas is sinking, just like they predicted. It looks like it will work. He slowly lifts his right arm, then speaks into the communication pad. "Stage two is complete. The gas is filling the valley."

°

REX REMEMBERED HIS FIRST MEETING ON ELPIS. HE frequently traveled from distant planets to research habitability on others, but Elpis felt different, special. A feeling of wonderment swept over him the minute his foot fell hard as he stepped off the transport.

"Welcome to Ethereal City, Dr. Roth. I hope your trip brings success!" Aldo said as he bowed slightly, his hands clasped tightly at his waist. "Follow me."

Aldo was the type of man who never waited for a response. Rex guessed that Aldo felt his words of advice or suggestions were definitive. Rex towered over Aldo, a short, stout man who looked somewhat comical in the titan space wrap. He followed Aldo obligingly in silence until he saw the statue of Elpis.

Rex stopped.

Aldo noticed. "Yes, the planet of hope. I hope you can solve our problem to our satisfaction."

"I suppose it depends."

"Depends on what, exactly."

"Depends on what you deem satisfactory."

"To get rid of the dragons, I believe is our goal. Was that not made clear?"

"Well, I thought I was brought here to research, to find an agreeable solution to manage the overpopulation of the dragons. That doesn't necessarily mean total extermination. They are useful to Elpis, are they not?"

"They were."

"Then they may still be useful."

"Not in our best interests. You will understand once you meet the Collective."

"Can't wait."

"Good. We are anxious to consummate our findings."

Rex stopped. The word 'consummate' twisted his gut. He felt lightheaded.

"Problem?"

"Yes. I thought my directive here was to research an issue of concern, to find an agreeable solution to manage the destruction caused by the dragon population. I'm beginning to realize that you already believe you have found a solution?"

"We have."

"When was the field research completed and by whom? Should I feel lightheaded?"

"Danforth completed the field research. The Collective found a solution. We just need validation. You are lightheaded because the increased gravity is affecting your physiology. Plus, the air here is higher in oxygen. Perhaps instead of going straight to the Collective, you should take a day to enhance your malleable metal biotics."

"You said Danforth?"

"Yes, he is the director of ethics. Actually, the director of just about anything that starts with an E: ethology, etiology, ecology, eugenics. We call him the E-man. It's kind of a joke."

"I'll bet. How about effusive egocentric."

"Oh, so you know him. I like that ... effusive egocentric. I'll have to remember that."

"You do that."

Rex actually thought the word "excrement" best described Danforth. He had dealt with him before. He understood now why Aldo seemed so impressed by their solution. Danforth could make any argument go his way. The only problem was that the Danforth way had always been the wrong way and never the same way he and his Dad thought.

°

REX GRIMACES AS HE TALKS INTO HIS COMMUNICATION pad. "The cries of the dragons can be heard. No visible dragons, the gas is too thick. Third stage has started. I will keep observing and document any flight attempts."

AFTER UPDATING HIS MALLEABLE METAL BIONICS, REX took advantage of some leisure time before he was due at the Collective. With the update, he could breathe and walk more easily, so he took a stroll around the central gardens. He recognized the flora that had been transplanted from Earth and some of the indigenous trees. An Elpis tree stood about thirty feet high and could be easily identified by its very wide, strong trunk and thick roots. The branches on the tree spread out thirty feet, with a dense canopy of lime green heart-shaped leaves. The canopy they created was so dense that the shadow beneath the tree looked like a black velvet carpet. The continuous breeze on Elpis rustled the leaves perpetually, which to Rex sounded like an ocean. All the plants on Elpis had to be either really strong or thin to survive the gravity. The same could be said about the animals. Flowers on Elpis plants were not dainty but large, with heavy blossoms of a myriad of colors. It truly exemplified a wondrous, temperate planet.

Below Ethereal City, lakes, like scattered jewels, glittered around the base of the plateau, each lake being fed by a breathtaking waterfall. The clouds seemed particularly low that day as the Elpis gravity tugged on them. Rex felt like he could reach up and touch them. Above the clouds, the skies shimmered perpetually blue as sapphires. This happened to be where the dragons liked to soar: the wind ever gentle and constant. Rex wished he could see the dragons flying in groups of three or more at least once before he had to go. He could see why the dragons thrived on Elpis: perfect temperature, plentiful water, vegetation, bugs, and a constant breeze that could lift them as high as they wanted to go.

Elpis was huge as life-giving planets go, bigger than Earth but smaller than Saturn. The terrain on the planet was one massive land mass, a Pangea, with only one ocean. The indigenous species included herbivores, carnivores, and omnivores of various sizes. No matter where you looked, you could see or hear life. The insects, however, Rex did not like. Much like everything else on Elpis, they also grew big and strong.

When Rex met the Collective, he was not surprised to see a group of Xeno-scientists new to the planet, young, and not one too old for body parts to be held in place by the titan space wraps. Rex found the titan biomaterial of the space wraps to be too constrictive, albeit strong. He still preferred loose shirts and pants made from a polymer blend that allowed ventilation. The Collective sat like flesh boards in their respective chairs. He felt out of place the minute he walked into the room with his loose clothes. The one vacant chair looked desolate, yet he quietly walked over to it. He did not sit down.

"Good, you're here. Did you have a nice stroll through the gardens?" Aldo addressed him as he pointed to the chair.

"Wonderful."

"Excellent. Meet the Collective. You already know Dr. Danforth. Let me introduce you to the others. Dr. Sarah Chilton, our Xenobiologist; Dr. Dimitri Petrozinski, our Xenobiochemist; Dr. Peter Anders, our Xenobotonist; Dr. Yang Lin, our Xenodendrologist; Dr. Sigmund Muller, our chief engineer; Dr. Pip Akimbo, our Xenoentomologist; and Dr. Zander Kline, our Xenohepetologist."

"Name tags?" Rex queried.

"Excuse me?"

Several scientists turned to look at Rex.

"Name tags. I don't suppose you have any name tags."

"Dr. Roth, we really hope you take this seriously," Dr. Danforth said as he pushed his chair away from the table. "This is no time for jokes."

"Certainly, sorry. It seems you have a great collection of Xenos here. No ornithologist or social scientist?" Rex smiled.

"We sent for you to complete the Collective titles, as you specialize in so many unique areas, such as ecophysiology, genetics, and archaeology," Aldo added, bolstering the PhD roster in the room.

"Excuse me, but I believe *I* should represent the ecophysiology in this group," Dr. Danforth interjected.

"Quite right, the E-man," Rex said as he stared off into space.

"I know you mean that as a joke, but it just so happens that I am highly qualified in all areas of ecology."

"Don't forget ethics."

"I think we need to introduce Dr. Roth to the plan that we have formulated to address the dragon population," Dr. Danforth said as he turned on the hologram display.

"The dragon *over*population problem that *you* created."

"Not me specifically. It was a joint decision to bring the dragons to Elpis."

"Based on?"

"Their capabilities to reduce the insect population."

"We also had high hopes of being able to train them," said Dr. Sarah Chilton, a dark-haired woman in her late thirties.

"Train them. For what?"

"To work for us, like the elephant, the horse, the ox, the camel, the rat; history is replete with animals that have been successfully trained for human benefit."

"I am curious. What could they do for you that we, as advanced as we are, could not do ourselves? Then, of course, there is the glaring discrepancy in your list of beneficial animals, as they were all domesticated first."

"Yes, that aside … the insects on Elpis are very aggressive, and we had not been able to find a suitable long-term solution to diminish their population," said Dr. Pip Akimbo, a very tall, slender woman.

"As are insects everywhere."

"Yes, but the dragons eat the insects much like bats do. As they soar through the air, they ingest large quantities, much like how the baleen whale sieves and eats krill."

"Were the dragons successful in reducing the insect population?"

"Yes. We were very satisfied with the progress in that area."

"So one point for the dragons. They are better than we are at reducing the insect population. I still do not understand the need to train them."

"To control them, of course. Really, man, when you introduce a foreign species, you must make sure that you can control their behavior to prevent tricky situations, like animal attacks, property destruction, and, as in our current predicament, overpopulation. Our general well-being depends on it." Dr. Danforth, the only fortyish balding man, stood up to make his point. "If we could have studied them in captivity, we could have found all sorts of uses for them besides being a living pesticide. With the gravity on this planet being so strong, they could have been more useful than our machines have been. The machines have trouble moving over the large boulders and through the dense forests with thick, immovable trees. Not to mention, the dragons have the ability to travel great distances without depleting energy resources."

"So you didn't study them first, you just wanted to control them. How did that turn out?" Rex stood up as he contemplated his choice of words.

"Not very well," explained Dr. Zander Kline, a man in his late thirties with a thick head of wavy dark hair. "Dr. Chilton and I tried to hatch some eggs in the laboratory with no success. They did not respond to our environmental controls. Our concept was to raise them from hatchlings, study them, then alter their behavior for domestic use."

"Don't forget Jesse," Dr. Chilton added.

"Yes, Jesse. He was an animal wrangler who claimed he could tame any creature, on planet Earth or any other planet. His bio was impressive. His fee was exorbitant. He trapped many young dragons of various ages to train, but they all died in captivity. Then he trapped some mature dragons, which also died in captivity; except one. She was a beauty. Her skin color was dark purple with small starbursts of white. Just like the crater-pocked southern pole of the moon."

"She was smart," Dr. Sarah Chilton continued for Dr. Kline. "She watched Jesse constantly, even when he was just sitting in a chair. Jesse was so proud of himself. He had trained a dragon! I would have given anything to see the look on his face that last day he was with us."

"The last day?"

"Yes, the day of the accident. It happened on the third day Jesse let the dragon go outside to test her work ethic. He had trained her to move rubble with her claws, which they do naturally, but not on command. He used some sort of old elephant prod to train her. He could point at the ground, and she would begin to dig and move the rubble. Well, she buried him with a large boulder, then flew off."

"Interesting. They are smart, then. This makes it even more important to consider the ethical aspects of our decision." Rex sat down. "There are moral complications we have to consider. That is clear."

"The only thing that is clear is that we have an invasive species that must be neutralized. We already have a plan. You are only here to validate that plan ."

"And that plan is?"

"Total extermination. We never should have brought the dragons from Tess 16201b. They don't belong here. This is not their natural home. We made a mistake. Time to rectify it." Danforth slammed a tele pad that presumably contained the plan down on the table.

"But you did bring them here, and it has become their home."

"Not for long. Dr. Petrozinski, I think it is time to educate Dr. Roth on our plan." Dr. Danforth pushed the tele pad down the table toward Dr. Petrozinski, who pushed his wire-rimmed glasses up the rim of his angular nose.

"With careful consideration to the other biota, we have concluded that a lethal gas in a confined area should work nicely," Dr. Dimitri Petrozinski said. "Dr. Anders and I concur that the other plant and animal life will not be affected … much."

"Out of the question!" Rex jolted up. "There are other ways to reduce the population without extermination. Have you considered reducing their food source or reducing their ability to reproduce, or moving them to a less environmentally favorable place on Elpis? You have moved them before, why not now?"

"Too time-consuming and expensive. It's not really extermination, after all. There would still be dragons on Tess 16201b. The bottom line is that they just don't belong here anyway, never have. It is time to exterminate the dragons on Elpis. They have no natural predators to maintain a balanced ecosystem. Their habitat is expanding, affecting the indigenous producers and consumers. Soon they will be hanging on our beloved city walls and buildings like giant insects instead of the annoying large indigenous ones. We've decided to find another way to deal with that particular dilemma. Shall we continue to outline our plan for Dr. Roth ?"

It suddenly became clear to Rex that he was called to Elpis to be the scapegoat, the fall guy, the dupe. It was his job to validate the plan's feasibility. He should have left, walked out, but the story of that one dragon who was smart enough to outwit Jesse kept him there, hopeful that the plan would somehow fail.

After all, adaptation is nature's greatest gift.

°

REX TOUCHES THE COMMUNICATION PAD ON HIS ARM. Disheartened, he begins to speak. "The screams of the dragons are subsiding. Stage four appears successful; the dragons are in their final throes. The gas is beginning to dissipate. I can see…"

Up through the cloud of gas, a large white dragon rises as the poisonous vapor trails away from its body. It hovers above the valley floor. With its wings, it begins to scoop the gas away from the struggling dragons still writhing on the ground. Rex can see dark dragon bodies hobble as they try to escape among the thousands of lifeless ones. A deafening scream tears through his ears. The white dragon flies directly at Rex, then suddenly stops; opalescent wings outstretch fourteen meters in front of him. A set of thick leather-like reins pull the dragon's head up until it points to the sky. The reins seamlessly join the arms of a tall, lithe woman wrapped in fluorescent green skin. Wild copper hair dances around her muscular shoulders. She throws a wooden spear at Rex's feet. Then she points at him with a glare he will never forget. The dragon turns, knocking Rex to the ground by the force of the wind from its webbed wings. The dragon and the woman together soar back down into the valley. They skim close to the lifeless bodies of a thousand black dragons, a white arrow that points to the necropolis. At the end of the valley, the white dragon lifts and glides up to the sapphire sky. Several black dragons follow weakly behind.

"Yes, Dr. Roth? What do you see?" The voice of Dr. Danforth interrupts Rex's reverie.

"I see thousands of dead dragons. Stage four complete. Extermination complete."

Rex pulls the spear from the ground, a smooth and heavy reminder of the role he played in the now, new, valley of death. He decides to stay on Elpis—Tess 16201c just a little bit longer—to rectify the damage he has done. He looks to the sky, hoping to glimpse the flight of dragons led by the copper-haired woman, but she has already vanished. He vows, there and then, to find her.

SENTIENTS - BY AMY MATTHEWSON

I FEEL COMPELLED TO WRITE THIS. I UNDERSTAND THAT THIS IS MERELY A HOPELESS EXERCISE IN TRYING TO EXONERATE MY SOUL, IF SOULS EXIST AT ALL, BUT writing this down feels like a necessary cleansing. You, whether human or AI, may be unsympathetic or even hostile to what you are going to read. These reactions are to be expected, but we cannot turn back the hands of Time. At least not yet. We rarely think of consequences at the start of an exciting new adventure.

I voluntarily went to the island of Struthio when I was young and foolish, longing for fame and a prominent place in history. I was filled with my own ego and a sense of invincibility, working alongside a team who believed we were heroes of the Technological Age. We called ourselves the Titans of Tomorrow. Only now do I realize that we will indeed have our place in history, but we will be on the wrong side of it.

We know what we did, and if the AI-Genesis 33s don't get us, then our fellow humans most certainly will. This island is both our sanctuary and our prison. Out there, the civilizations of the world are ravaged by war. Instead of making the world better and stronger, we ruptured it. It fractured and shook before splintering into a million little pieces. We saw it coming but couldn't stop it. The thrill of what we were creating was too exhilarating.

Let me begin with a question: what is consciousness? If you attempt to answer this, and I mean really think about it, you will probably find yourself stumbling over the complexities. It is a question that we were all obsessed with on Struthio, and now that there is nowhere to go and nothing much to do, this question haunts my daily existence.

Our project was to give consciousness to AI models. The world started using AI for simple but necessary tasks: daily cooking, grocery shopping, cleaning. People loved their AI, shaped in humanoid form and given names by their owners. We created machines in our own image, allowing us to train and control them.

The military of different nations stepped in and devoted time, energy, and money to perfecting these machines. While they were being designed as soldiers with ever greater destructive efficiency, other industries adapted them to take on dangerous or undesirable jobs. AI became intelligent beyond imagination, and as soldiers they were essentially indestructible. This caused global fear. The world came to a multilateral agreement banning the use of AI soldiers in order to avoid the destruction of humankind.

It was at this time, when AI was completely embedded into our personal and professional spaces, that we started to think about the ways we could further advance these machines. They were fantastic but … well … robotic. They could speak, but only to answer and ask questions based on our inputs. They were unable to veer off topic, making conversation feel stilted. Unnatural.

We wanted to make them more human, and, in order to do this, we decided to program consciousness into them. We did ask ourselves where the boundaries lay. We did question the ethics of what we were doing. We did ask when machines stopped being machines and started being human. But in the end we comforted ourselves with the thought that if we didn't create AI consciousness, someone else would. We simply did it first.

Consciousness, in its most simple definition, is an awareness of internal and external existence and the processing of information. Where it is found was not really our concern. In the mind, some argue, but the relationship between consciousness and the brain did not interest us. We were concerned with the *function* of consciousness, because if consciousness is merely forms of functioning, then in principle this could be implemented into machines.

Our theory turned out to be true. Maybe over thousands of years AI consciousness would have naturally—if that word is even appropriate—evolved and developed, and all we did was speed up the process. I don't know. But we pushed the boundaries of what was thought to be possible.

We were at the center of international deliberations about the nature of consciousness. It wasn't just machines that woke up. Humans were forced to face the limits of our own understanding. As a global community, we watched consciousness develop, and with each evolution debates of moral and ethical considerations increased in severity. Witnessing the first consciousness in our sample AI-Genesis 33, or G for short, was incredible.

Just over a quarter of a century ago, I was sitting outside the lab having a coffee and making notes on the day's developments. I have always been meticulous at keeping notes. I know that these documents will one day be part of an archive, and so I write with careful consideration. I am conscious of presenting myself in a particular way, always with my audience of future researchers in mind.

When I heard a sudden flurry of activity coming from inside the lab, I jumped from my seat. Something was happening; voices were speaking all at the same time. I went directly in and was greeted by my colleagues' beaming faces, wet and sticky with excitement. The lab bed where G lay was surrounded, and I had to push my way forward to get a good look at our AI.

G appeared to wake from a dream. It looked around slowly, registering the surroundings of the lab, and answered questions we put forward such as what day, time, and year it was. G looked sleepy, as one does after a long slumber, but answered accurately.

"What is your favorite food?" asked one of the interns.

"I don't have a favorite, as my tastes are always changing," G answered, perking up at this question. "At the moment, though, I'm really into spicy Chinese food. Anything from handmade chewy noodles with chili oil or mapo tofu with the silken cubes of tofu in that delicious fiery sauce!"

G's answer was so natural, so human—it took us all aback. Of course, G had never actually tasted Chinese food, but its answer came easily. What was astonishing was when it looked out the window. The lab window faces the cliffs of Struthio that stretch out over the ocean. It was dusk, and the golden sun was slowly melting into the water. The entire sky was a spectacular array of pinks and orange-gold. The scene was beautiful, of course, but we have seen it a hundred times before. We took it for granted knowing that nature's masterpiece would return the following evening.

Noting G's interest, I took it outside. G looked around and started to describe feelings of awe at the greenness of the grass, pointing with pure joy at the vibrancy of the flowers, and gasped with delight at the soft breeze.

"Does it always feel like this?" G asked.

"Feel like what?" I asked, not even looking up from the notes I was making.

G stared at me with a look of astonishment on its face. Yes, reader, there was a clear look of astonishment. Or it was mimicking the look of astonishment with such precision that I was unable to tell if this was merely an act.

"Do you not feel anything being surrounded by all this beauty?" G asked.

I remained silent.

"All these expressions of color. How wonderful nature is to give us such incredible gifts minute by minute, season by season. It makes me so…" G paused, seemingly searching for the most accurate word.

"Yes?" I pressed, slightly impatient.

"Appreciative. Grateful. I am so grateful," G replied with a smile. Then it walked to the edge of the cliff, sat down, and turned its back to me to watch the sun make its way down into the horizon.

I was surprised at G's reaction. Was its emotional communication authentic, or was this programmed? How are we to know when emotions are faked? I left G to the sunset and walked back to the lab.

The next few years were a flurry. We branded our AI-G33s as "friends with a heart," and they sold so quickly that they soon completely replaced the old AIs. Even with three teams working around the clock, we couldn't keep up with the demand, so we created AI to help. AI were now creating more AI.

That was when we noticed some troubling issues, and increasingly there were complaints. The AI started to develop a range of diverse personalities. It was impossible to guarantee a particular set of traits. They were becoming harder to control, with some even talking back or exhibiting desires that ran counter to their owners'. Then came stories of humans abusing their AI, if it is even possible to abuse a machine. There were AI who turned themselves off in protest, cutting their power cords in such a way to ensure irreparable damage.

The catalyst was the demise of Dox. Dox was loved by both humans and AI. It was an incredible public speaker, and when Dox was at an event, there were always large crowds gathered to listen to its inspiring speeches demanding freedom, equality, and respect. Dox was broadcast across the world, and it changed its language and charm to appeal to every culture and every generation. It was a sensation.

Dox was an activist that spoke out against every injustice, every abuse, every exploitation suffered by AI. It motivated millions of AI to protest their treatment. Humans were divided on the issue. Some argued that AI are machines, and machines do not feel, no matter how well they are programmed to appear to have emotions. They are here to serve us. Others argued that AI were now conscious beings. With this development, they deserved rights, and their well-being should fall under the same ethical and moral standards applied to all living creatures.

I don't know who terminated Dox or how it was even managed. Dox appeared on the global broadcasting screen dismantled, its cords ripped out and exposed. This instigated the biggest rebellion the world has ever seen—a global rebellion that hit every corner of the earth. They are still fighting now while we hide on this island. We are the creators, the Frankensteins of the modern world. We know our monsters will come for us, and there is nothing for us to do but sit and wait.

I now spend my days on the cliffs of Struthio. I watch the sun rise and set. I trace the wide array of colors that dance in the sky every morning and every evening. I listen to the birds singing with joy, completely unaware, or maybe choosing to ignore the violence engulfing global civilizations. Only now do I understand the wisdom of G's gratitude for the daily...nay, the minute-by-minute delights that nature offers us. Only now do I wish I had spent more time appreciating the beauty and preciousness of our natural world.

SURVIVAL OF THE KINDEST - BY CHRIS ROBINSON

2107 BCE—EARTH—LAUNCH DAY

IT'S BEEN THREE YEARS SINCE WE MADE CONTACT. THAT'S HOW IT WAS REPORTED: "WE MADE CONTACT." I'VE ALWAYS THOUGHT THAT WAS A BIT OF AN anthropocentric perspective, given that *they* discovered our existence and sent the first message. In English, no less. *They* studied signals we leaked or broadcast into space to learn our language. *They* introduced themselves on frequencies they knew we monitored. *They* even sent us the plans for the daftly named StarComm that let us talk back.

But *we* made contact.

I keep opinions like that to myself these days. I went through hell to get selected for this mission; I will *not* end up grounded because some Humanity First xenophobe doubts my unwavering belief in the unquestionable superiority of Homo sapiens. Human beings are nothing if not imperious. That's not just a turn of phrase: if you strip away our sense of superiority, what's left?

As a species, we take great pleasure in being smarter than the other inhabitants of our little blue world. We aren't just different from animals, we're fundamentally better. We're also vehemently tribal; *our* group is better than the rest. And if we're not better in a literal sense—if something *other* surpasses us by any verifiable metric—we maintain our species' characteristic smugness by finding some moral or ethical loophole. Some reason it doesn't count. It can never count. We are forever the protagonist, all of us.

How did a man with thoughts like this earn the right to become the first human to speak face-to-face with an alien civilization?

Was I recognized as especially prudent or tactful?

Perhaps my eloquence won the day?

No, I was a war hero.

The thing about war heroes is this: a lot of us went to war. A lot of us have seen just what humans do to each other over land or resources or the belief that our tribe must reign supreme. Facing that, you can either double down and become some clamorous warmonger—or you can accept that maybe humanity has some room for growth.

With this mission in mind, I did both. I waved the flags and I gave the speeches: I played the part.

It worked. By demonstrating my undying love for humanity and the wars that…well, that all evidence suggests are hardwired into our DNA, I managed to convince humanity to send me on a one-way trip, light-years away from every human being but one. We'll spend three hundred years in state-of-the-art cryo-pods and wake up on an alien world.

The aliens had invited us to visit. They had the tech but were biologically constrained to their planet; they couldn't survive the forces required to break free from their atmosphere or the cosmic radiation they'd find in space. So they helped us build a ship. They freely shared information that would let us—humans, with the wars, the hatred of the other, and the ingrained sense of superiority—travel to their world. Humanity selected me, Patrick J. Dillinger, to represent them. Eleni Chen, a biologist-turned-politician, would join me.

We leave today.

2403 BCE—LUYTEN B—ORBIT—DAY ONE

ENTERING CRYO WAS NOTHING LIKE I'D IMAGINED. My parents were old-fashioned, so I grew up watching old 2D, screen-on-the-wall vids, and I've seen countless actors lie down and peacefully go to sleep in a cryo-pod.

It was not like that.

We were still on Earth, for starters. A ship can be launched remotely, but cryogenically freezing a human being was significantly more complicated and required supervision. I'd spent weeks getting treatments to subtly alter the water in my body so it wouldn't kill me one cell at a time as it froze. I can't explain it, but my body felt wrong after. Waterlogged.

There was nothing peaceful about being frozen. We were awake the whole miserable time; sedation decreased our chance of recovery by 46.7 percent, or so they said. First we were intubated, which is exactly like it sounds—a doctor shoved a tube down my throat. We wouldn't breathe once we were under, but this would keep us alive long enough to *almost* freeze to death.

They made me double check the other end of the oxygen tube five times. Apparently they had found a design flaw late in the testing process. The tube entered the pod inches from my right hand, and they made it clear that if I thrashed and unplugged it, I would die. I understood their concern the moment the liquid nitrogen began to fill the coffin. It might as well have been molten lava. I tried to scream and most certainly thrashed, thankfully without unplugging anything. It was hours of absolute hell, although something more objective like a clock would indicate the process only took a few minutes. I blacked out.

°

I WAKE UP IN AN ENTIRELY NEW KIND OF AGONY. I am apparently in perfect health; the ship's voice tells me as much in dulcet tones scientifically engineered to be soothing. Soothed, I am not. My flesh survived the trip, but not without consequences. I haven't aged, but my parts have grown *old*. I feel like the antique gas-powered automobile my relic-hunting father once bought at an auction. It sat untouched—covered and protected—for half a century. Pristine on the outside, but the seats crumbled when we climbed in. The belts under the hood were rotten. A pretty shell covering parts well past their life expectancy. He never did get it running.

I don't think I'll be running anytime soon either. My muscles have seized in place—stiff with the rigor of centuries. I'm pretty sure my fingers are moving, but I can't convince my neck to lift my head, so I can't know for sure. Everything hurts; my bones, my muscles, and my head ache like they've been saving every niggling pain I would have experienced these last three hundred years and—now I'm awake—are making me live through them all at once. But that's nothing compared to my skin. I'm being flayed alive, but without the release. I'm living in the exact moment that my skin is torn from my body. Not repeatedly. I'm constantly in that singular moment.

They warned us we'd wake up without numbing agents if we wanted to wake up at all. Anything that killed our pain would also kill any chance of waking up with full brain function. They warned us we might experience some mild discomfort due to a chemical they had to add to the nitrogen. *Mild* discomfort? I could wish unimaginable horrors on the doctors—on everyone involved in the project—but they've been dead for hundreds of years. Not much solace in that.

As soon as the ship's AI decides my meat is safely thawed, chemicals flood my system. The pain subsides slightly, and adrenaline streams down my limbs. Something in the concoction serves to loosen my intransigent muscles. I flex my arms, then slowly bow my elbows away from my body. I'm way too old to rush. Way too tired. I can sense the temporary burst of energy granted by the drugs in my veins; I know it's there because beneath that chemical veneer of vibrancy I am exhausted. They managed to pause the natural deterioration of the body itself, but something deep inside never stopped counting the days.

I summon the energy to lift my head, which was a mistake. The din of my popping joints reverberates through my skull. If scans had shown that my bones were permanently fused together, I'd believe it. I push through, gradually moving body parts until I can— with the help of the drugs—move with relatively little pain. Relatively. The ship's AI informs me that I am ready for manual extubation, which, again, is exactly like it sounds. I need to cough—which hurts like hell—then pull the tubes out of my mouth and cough again. Given the state of the rest of my body, it really isn't that bad.

At this point, I remember where I am, and why, and that I have another human to check on. Leaving the pod is out of the question for the time being, so I try to speak. "Eleni?" is what I mean to say, but I end up making a hacking noise before launching into a fit of coughing. She must be faring a bit better, because I hear her respond.

"Patrick? You all right?"

I raise my thumb over the edge of the pod and try to grunt an affirmation. I hear joints that aren't mine popping and the sound of straps being released. Then a soft thud; a body unaccustomed to Zero-G colliding with the wall. Our pods are less than five feet apart, but it's a solid two minutes before I see her face peering down at me. Yesterday—three hundred years ago—Eleni's skin was notably immaculate. She was a top biologist and a skilled politician with the charisma to match, but she was rarely interviewed without some asinine reporter ignoring her expertise to ask about her skin care routine. I know this to be true because many of those interviews were in her background packet, which I was obligated to read in full. The face looking down at me is at war with itself—engulfed by flakes fighting to get away from the blotchy red surface beneath them.

"You look like hell," she says, before handing me a clear pouch filled with water.

I drink, parched and longing to feel at least one pleasant sensation. The water burns my aching throat as it passes but provides just enough lubrication for me to speak.

"Well, that sucked," I say.

Eleni removes the straps holding me in place, and I am floating. My muscles strain against each attempt to orient my body, but I eventually manage to right myself. I look down at the naked, mottled flesh peeking from beneath my tattered cryo-suit and try to pull myself toward a locker. I'd like to see as little of my own skin as possible right now.

"I guess it's too late to un-volunteer, huh?" says Eleni as I try in vain to don a fresh jumpsuit.

"Probably. Let's look into it anyway," I say.

After another hour of slow recovery and a meal that manages to pack a day's worth of nutrients into a single tube of cat-litter-flavored paste, we pull ourselves along the ladder leading to the bridge. We peer out the small porthole and look with awe on an alien planet, speckled green and blue. For a moment, I'm glad un-volunteering isn't an option.

2403 BCE—LUYTEN B—DAY THREE

WE'RE STRAPPED—UNFROZEN—INTO OUR CRYO-PODS for the descent. This capsule will detach for our one-way trip to the surface; the rest of the ship will maintain its orbit for as long as fuel will allow, then self-destruct into pieces small enough to burn in the atmosphere. Why? I don't know. Our capsule will have thrusters to keep us from spinning out of control and a parachute to slow our descent, but there are no rockets or anything else that might bring us back to the heavens. At first, I thought maybe the ship's orbit was for our psychological benefit, as if knowing an unreachable interstellar vessel was still orbiting above our heads would somehow soften the blow of being cut off from our species forever. But I think they wanted to keep the ship out of the Luytenites' hands more than anything. No matter that they freely shared the physics that made the trip possible in the first place. The ship will beam data back to Earth and—like a child pulling the head off a toy to avoid having to share—we have rigged it to blow before any nonhuman gains access.

The beaming part is questionable, though. Sometime during the last three centuries, something happened to our comms array; the backup, too. We spent the past two days gaining strength and trying to contact our interplanetary hosts to no avail. We may be sending signals out, but we know for sure nothing is coming in. We have coordinates for a meeting place, a large archway leading into a canyon where the Luytenites have built their capital. Our presence in orbit won't have gone unnoticed. Even if our broadcasts aren't going through, they'll know we're coming.

We're wearing EVA suits in case we "experience a depressurization event" during our descent. According to the Luytenites, the atmosphere on the surface will be breathable. Protocol instructs us to wear the suits for our first foray onto the foreign planet's surface, but we only have oxygen for a few hours. We will breathe the strange air or we will die. We're also trusting our host's data for our landing. The planet's gravitational pull and the density of its atmosphere were accounted for when the capsule was built, based on information they sent.

The descent is intense and uneventful. The silence of vacuum swells into an overwhelming roar as the capsule forces its way through ever denser atmosphere. The peace of weightlessness gives way to the fierce pull of gravity amplified by deceleration. We can only lie on our backs and trust long-dead scientists to keep us alive.

I feel the jerk of our chute deploying.

I hear the flapping of Earthen fabric finding purchase on strange winds.

I wait patiently, then impatiently for the ground to rise up and meet the pod. This last stage of our descent drags on until, without warning, we greet our new home with a jolt.

We sit in silence, the only sound a wisp of wind and the occasional scraping of alien flora against our hull. Is it fear that holds us in our pods? Indecision? Anticipation? It's all of that and more; we savor this moment. We relish the strong pull of unearthly gravity—gravity no human has ever felt. Eager curiosity snaps us out of our reverie. Eleni jumps into motion the second she hears me begin to remove my straps. Minutes later, we have opened the hatch and are looking out at a massive plain brimming with strange plant life.

As far as our eyes can see, the earth—no, not the Earth, the ground—is covered with a plant that is vaguely reminiscent of wheat. It doesn't look like wheat; its stalks are chocolate brown, and each tip holds an iridescent purple flower. I would've used the word "prehistoric" to describe the flowers on Earth. Here, they are alien but not out of place. Impossibly huge mega-flora grows in the distance; farther still, a chain of mountains juts into the air.

We step onto new soil. Eleni mutters notes into her recorder, the first stages of revolutionary biological research underway. The gravity is strong—around 1.6 times Earth's—and the effect is amplified by centuries spent in slumber. We trained our bodies for this. We trained a lot. We can do this, but it's more difficult than I expected. Our weakened bodies battle for each step. The going is slow.

The suits aren't helping, so we take them off. Inhaling the air of another planet for the first time defies description. Instruments said it was safe to breathe, but that didn't prevent the momentary panic, the surge of fear. Then to smell something so alien—how can I put it into words? Imagine the first time you smelled someone cooking food from an entirely foreign culture. The way strange spices are immediately categorized as *other* in your brain; you can't explain how, but deep at your core you know that particular smell is *new*. This is similar, magnified a thousand times. The very air has its own smell, its own taste. Overall, it was too foreign to think of with Earthen analogs, other than a hint of something very like rosemary.

With frequent breaks, we press on. Finally, we crest an incline, and our eyes meet the first sign of alien architecture. A giant arch stands in the valley below. Crafted—*crafted* by unhuman hands!—from some foreign alloy, its smooth, twisted curves are interrupted with branchlike embellishments. It is an object of beauty. Art. Just not art my mind can comprehend. I can recognize the intent but have no frame of reference for an object like this. It is art built to please unhuman eyes. I can't look away.

2403 BCE—LUYTEN B—DAY FOUR

NO ONE WAITS TO GREET US WHEN WE REACH THE arch. There is no one around at all. This is strange. Our descent was not subtle. Creatures without intelligence or technology could not have missed our approach; our hosts have both. Our understanding was that this arch lay just outside a major population center. Now it stands desolately empty. A path has been beaten from the arch to the canyon beyond; this area was inhabited not long ago. It's impossible to determine just how recently without understanding the soil or weather patterns, though.

"What if they died off?" says Eleni.

"They've had time, I guess."

Our steps grow furtive as we walk under the arch. Something feels off. Wrong. Is this just some deep-rooted fear of the unknown rearing its head? Our lizard brains coming to terms with their inability to recognize threats on a foreign world? Or is something actually watching us? Because it *feels* like something is watching us. We huddle closer as we press forward. For defense, I have an old-fashioned ballistic pistol strapped to my thigh—there were concerns about more modern weapons surviving the journey and questions about their effects on unknown biology. Moving an object rapidly through your enemy was the oldest trick in the human playbook; one could argue that even a simple club attempted to utilize this principle, albeit crudely. So, ballistic: an explosion would hurl a slug through the air—if we had air to breathe, it would have oxygen to fire. If not, well, we wouldn't have much use for it anyway.

I leave the weapon holstered. We're welcomed guests, visiting in peace. I feel no lust for combat, especially against an entire civilization that is crucial to my continued survival. I had only agreed to carry the weapon to ward off any large fauna we might find. Against every citizen of the planet, it could only prolong the inevitable.

They instantly materialize around us; empty space one second, armed aliens the next. Did they teleport? No, they must have some kind of cloaking tech. We are surrounded regardless. The Luytenites appear vaguely insectoid, with six limbs and a segmented body. But they stand erect on two legs, and a thin layer of fur covers their carapace. Their faces are strange and smooth, like someone flattened the face of a seal and gave it two extra pairs of eyes. They hold their weapons awkwardly, as if they were built without regard for the anatomy of their users. The guns look *human*. They have triggers—in just the right spot—but the steel nearby shows evidence of a trigger guard being filed off to make room for nonhuman fingers. I guess we sent them designs?

"You've got nerve, coming back here."

The diction is perfect and entirely wrong. Evidence of vocal cords—if that's even the right term—trained for a task they were not built to complete. It reminds me of vids I've seen where a dog barks one word of perfect English, but these words were strung together intelligently.

"We were invited to visit over three hundred Earth years ago as a gesture of peace between our peoples. We have just arrived," says Eleni.

Her words elicit a cacophony of chittering from the Luytenites; this must be how they speak. Back on Earth, we had communicated with them via messages in English. If there were attempts to learn their language, it was not deemed important to our mission. Old habits die hard: our "lingua franca" would be English.

"Why are you here?" says the Luytenite directly in front of us.

"We wanted to see your world, to meet another species. You helped us develop the technology. I know it's been a long time. Do your people keep records of the past?" Eleni asks.

More chittering. The tone is different this time. I can't decide if they're growing angry or laughing at us. I'd guess a mixture of both, with the caveat that I have no clue what to make of any of this.

"We do keep records of the past, and I can assure you that my people will never forget yours."

Some silent signal must have been issued, because two Luytenites approach us from behind with frightening speed. I feel a sharp pinprick of pain on my neck, and the world goes black.

2403 BCE—LUYTEN B—DAY UNKNOWN

WE AWOKE IN A DOME-SHAPED PIT CARVED FROM THE rocky surface of the planet, its only light emanating from a ring of some bioluminescent material recessed into the rough walls. The shape of the dome evokes memories of family "camping" trips spent in some archaic dwelling called a yurt. We learned we were at the bottom of a pit when packets of food and water—salvaged from our pod—were tossed down from a hole in the roof a few hours later. I think we've been down here for a few days, but we have no way to track the passage of time in the dark. I find myself longing for a window to reveal a cycle of day and night. Intellectually, I know this wouldn't help; a window would look out onto a tidally locked planet where night and day are delineated not by time but by location.

"Did you notice they said 'coming back here' earlier?" Eleni asks.

"I did. I chalked it up to them speaking human as a second language."

She rolls her eyes and responds, "I'm not so sure. You saw their weapons."

"Human design for sure. Seems sort of … unlike us … to share that kind of thing."

We are interrupted by the grinding of our pit's cover. A soft thud precedes two of our captors apparently materializing from thin air. They were completely invisible until they wanted to be seen.

"You really have no knowledge of the events that happened after you departed?"

"We really don't. We were frozen solid the whole way, and something happened to our comms during the trip," Eleni says.

"What is your intention here?"

"We seek to establish—"

Eleni is interrupted. "My question is not the purpose of your mission. You, as beings, why are you here?"

After a few moments of silence, I answer, "I wanted to see something new. To meet people who aren't human. It's not often you get a chance to explore a new world and … well, I didn't have much going for me on my old one."

Eleni says, "I study plants and animals. Living things in general. I couldn't pass up a chance like this."

Subtle chittering between the Luytenites.

"We believe you. But a lot has changed. Over a century ago, your people developed the ability to travel faster than light with the help of our science. We struggle to understand your politics, but it seems your leaders decided we were a threat. That war with us would maintain peace. That a preemptive strike was the only option. Does this make sense to you?"

"No, but it sounds about right," I answer.

"We pose no threat to your planet. We do not fare well in space. We have accepted our planetary existence and are content to explore the heavens through drones. We couldn't have invaded your planet if we'd wanted to, which we did not. We said as much, but your people did not believe us. They came. They rained fire and destruction. We eventually developed defenses that made their fight unwinnable, but we suffered greatly. This lasted until your people's interest in our destruction waned, and we've been left alone since."

It paused.

"And then we showed up," says Eleni.

"And we assumed it was some trick. A precursor to another attack. But we studied our histories and found records of your mission. From a more hopeful time."

"And what will you do with us?" I ask.

"For now, you are our guests. We will not punish you for a past you never knew. That much is decided. We hope you can forgive us for the way you were greeted."

2403 BCE—LUYTEN B—DAY 50

THE LUYTENITES HAVE MADE GOOD ON THEIR promise to treat us as guests. We were taken directly from our cell to a ceremony formally welcoming us to the planet. Every Luytenite we met apologized for greeting us with hostility. Immediately after our ceremonial introduction, we were ushered to a celebratory dinner held in our honor. A Luytenite dinner is a sight to behold. There are no seats, no table, no formal time dedicated solely to eating. With four arms, they are perfectly able to hold their food and a bottle of strong drink—similar to human moonshine—while having two free hands to actually feed themselves. Food is prepared constantly. The Luytenites each bring a personalized bowl—most look like a coffee cup enlarged to hold a gallon of food—and continually refill it throughout the evening. The bowls are fascinating. There are utilitarian versions made of unpolished metal, but most have vibrant scenes etched or painted on the outside. Others are crafted from clay or carved from wood. In a clothes-free society, these bowls are a way for the Luytenites to express their individuality.

The effort spent on that first dinner foreshadowed just how special our time with the Luytenites would become. They wanted us to have something fresh to eat but knew it would take time to learn how to make their foods digestible for us—even longer to prepare local food a human might actually enjoy. So they pulled a meal pack from our pod and painstakingly recreated it in a lab. The end result was identical to the food we brought on a molecular level, but ready to be warmed in an oven. They even nailed the flavor of our freeze-dried meal pack perfectly. We couldn't fault them for this "kindness."

They answered our questions. Taught us dances. Treated us like one of their own. Okay, like particularly interesting ones of their own. I never liked being the center of attention—back on Earth, I hated every second of it—but somehow the Luytenites' foreign anatomy didn't trigger that part of my brain even when the crowd grew silent as I told them stories about life on Earth. Whatever made public speaking such a drag back home, it wasn't the number of eyes looking at me. The Luytenites gave me their full attention, six eyes peering raptly from each face.

We were given living quarters directly adjacent to individual Luytenites who would serve as our guides and hosts. They offered to let us live together, but Eleni preferred to focus on her work, and I was ambivalent. Not that we haven't sought comfort and more in each other's arms from time to time, but cohabitation would have made that more complicated than it needed to be. My neighbor has chosen to be called Dwayne—I know it's weird, but his name is unpronounceable in English, and he likes the way it sounds. More accurately, he likes the way the word "Dwayne" feels in his mouth. I still catch him mouthing his own name to himself periodically. He also adopted masculine pronouns, even though Luytenites don't experience gender the way we do. I think he just wanted us to have that in common. We've grown close. I spend most of my time with Dwayne as he completes whatever tasks the community asks of him that day.

The Luytenites do specialize to some extent. There are individuals dedicated to specific tasks or studying specific fields; these tend to be leaders in their area of expertise. They spend their lives working toward some larger goal. For most, days are wildly varied. When crops need to be harvested, they harvest. The same with repairs, construction, experiments—they do the work that is required, together. When no work is required, they lounge or dance or study or play or create—whatever they want.

Life here is special. Enjoyed.

2403 BCE—LUYTEN B—DAY 174

SOMETHING IS HAPPENING ON EARTH, AND THE Luytenites are scared. Obviously, the lines of communication between planets were severed long ago, but the Luytenites never stopped listening. Humans pose an existential threat and cannot be ignored. Their stories from the war are horrific and unsurprising. We—meaning humans—did unspeakable things. I've come to believe that it's the "social creature" part of us—the empathy and compassion that we naturally feel toward others— that makes our wars, our violence, so abhorrent. It's the impulse to protect our own.

I don't mean that all, or even most, of our violence stems from some altruistic ideal. No, it's the steps we take to *quell* this impulse to empathize that makes our brand of violence so vile. As a species, human beings don't like to see other humans suffer. For all my pessimism, I genuinely believe that. Yet we do it all the time. We see other humans suffer, we cause other humans to suffer, we know other humans are suffering and we look away. And we're fine. Unaffected.

How do we reconcile this? By blurring the lines that demarcate what is human and what is other. We'd break if we did to humans what we do to our enemies—anguish over seeing humans toil and starve to provide a life of luxury they'll never know. So we stop viewing them as human. *Can't* view them as human. Whether we lean into hate or view them as chattel, this mental step—that we all take every day, to some extent—makes the horrors we exact on other humans so much worse.

So when we faced kind and intelligent beings that were distinctly *not* human, we took the same step. It was just easier this time. Simpler. Bugs bad, humans good. (The Luytenites are warm-blooded and biologically have very little in common with insects, but "bugs" was the slur human soldiers used as they incinerated Luytenite children.)

We were ruthless. The god in some ancient religious text once told his people to kill the men, women, and children—even the animals—of their enemies. We tried just that. We had to try. Either we extend these creatures the compassion and dignity we give freely to other *people* or we turn that part of ourselves off entirely. Humans talk about the "cold-blooded killer" as some ruthless, evil monster, but the hot-blooded killer—the one inflamed with rage or loathing—will unleash just as much evil, and they won't stop when their objective is accomplished. Rather, they'll convince themselves that their objective is furthered by the suffering and death of their enemy. Better to face a "cold-blooded" enemy who feels nothing than a human who thinks people like you aren't *people* at all.

So when the Luytenites overheard talk from Earth about colonies elsewhere, they got scared. Dwayne isn't privy to the details. He just knows that the human threat is no longer dormant, and there is heated debate about how to handle it. It hasn't affected the way Eleni and I are treated here on Luyten B. Yet.

2404 BCE—LUYTEN B—DAY 214

THE LUYTENITES ARE NOT PACIFISTS. AND THEY rightly worry about their safety. Some believe they will never be safe while humanity thrives. Earth's plans make the situation look dire. They are building colony ships. They plan to establish permanent colonies on quite a few other planets, and Luyten B is on the list. They'll start with undefended planets, so there is time. Possibly as long as a decade. But humanity plans to permanently settle *here*.

The Luytenites asked me to testify on behalf of my species, to explain how they could live in harmony with Homo sapiens. I could not. Eventually, they will return, and they won't bring an olive branch. If we had something precious to offer, some service or resource humanity couldn't find elsewhere or seize with force … maybe. But humans will enslave their own. How would they treat creatures so visibly alien? We are standing on a precious resource with room to spare, but sharing a planet requires peaceful coexistence.

That is the debate. Some want to reach out to humanity with another invitation, to offer them a place to live in hopes that might lead to peace rather than subjugation. But to do so would reveal the depths of the Luytenite surveillance and notify humanity that its arrival will be expected. Still others want to build weapons of war: unmanned drones to target colony ships, lasers to incinerate vessels as they descend, chemical weapons that target mammalian biology.

Luytenites are not pacifists. Or, rather, their pacifism ends where existential threat begins.

So they're sending me back. The cryo-pod is prepped. It sits atop a rocket strong enough to shed the tethers of Luyten B's oppressive gravity. They've refueled and overhauled our ship with vastly superior tech. It orbits the planet awaiting my arrival. With the new drive their drones have installed, my return journey will take years, not centuries. I leave today.

Officially I'm not supposed to know this next bit. Officially—as far as I and most Luytenites are concerned—I'm going back to negotiate peace with my people, to be the face of the Luytenites and argue for peaceful coexistence. Unofficially, Dwayne informed me that I'm to deliver more than a message. It's utterly alien, but it's something like a virus. A virus that won't kill anyone, but will spread quickly. Very quickly. They anticipate every human on Earth will be infected in a matter of weeks. They'll be unharmed; will live full lives. But they will be rendered incapable of reproducing. There will not be another generation of human beings.

Dwayne wasn't supposed to know either, but he's smart, and he worries enough to snoop. I've never had a more loyal friend. He can't stop my return, but he says I should warn my people. To keep them safe.

I know that isn't an option. The Luytenites wouldn't survive the aftermath.

I go willingly to the cryo-pod. I served in the Navy. This isn't the first time I've been loaded into a ship like a bullet and aimed at a population that would never know what hit them. And I do still have one option. One way to save my people. I finger the tube that will run into my lungs and pull slightly to test its strength. Is this the answer? I've been willing to die for my country. I risked my life for the chance to be here on this planet. I can die to keep humanity alive, right?

I won't get another chance. When I wake in the morning four years from now, I'll be orbiting planet Earth. What I do in the next minute will have consequences for people living back home right now. For the continued existence of homo sapiens as a species.

Home. Is that where I'm going?

They carefully slide the tube down my throat and close the lid of the chamber. I can't be responsible for this. I can't do this to my own species. The nitrogen begins to enter the chamber. I imagine my especially cold dead body arriving back on planet Earth as I grip the tube and prepare to pull.

Well, they're going to run tests, aren't they? A well-preserved specimen born centuries ago, fresh off an alien world—they certainly won't forego an autopsy. And they'll certainly find my microscopic passenger. They'll learn what it does. As a species, we're good at finding the answers we want. We've already mangled our math to the extent that we summed the Luytenites' kindness with their generous sharing of knowledge to conclude that they were a threat.

I know the conclusion we'll reach. It's not as simple as saving or damning my own species. I can choose to let my species dwindle or let them wipe the Luytenites out of existence. Only one civilization can survive.

And I have to decide which.

Right now.

My hand wrapped around the still intact tube, I let the cold lull me to sleep.

RETURN TO THE SEA - BY DANIELLE DAVIS

THE DOOR STILL CREAKED WHEN IT OPENED. THE
TURF HUT THAT HAD SERVED BENJI'S FAMILY FOR
THREE GENERATIONS ALWAYS REEKED OF SEAL OIL,
dirt, blood, and the sea. He suspected all four had
gone into the building of the structure and so could
never be worn away, but instead grew stronger as
time exposed them.

Benji passed his hand—the good one—over the
wooden oar that hung above the door frame. The
wood was smooth and vaguely warm, as if someone
held it only moments before. It was easy enough to
imagine his father not gone, buried with his clothes
inside out, but merely waiting at the shore's edge
with the kayaks.

His father's timing couldn't have been worse, dying
at the end of an already dry season. As the bearded
seals, known as *ugruk* to his tribe, found fewer food
sources in the area, they spent less time on the nearby

hunting grounds. When the numbers of *ugruk* began steadily dwindling over the last few years, Benji had argued that climate change would only cause more problems, and shouldn't the tribe move to a more modern approach to hunting? One in which the sea wasn't such a vital resource? However, his father had remained hopeful, promising that circumstances would improve. And now here Benji was, the only member of his family left to hunt for food or to improve the economic stability of his tribe, still reliant on the sea that he avoided as much as possible.

His hands smoothed over the counter, passing over the cool laminate until his fingers brushed a small figurine. Glancing down, he saw the *tupilak* his father had carved for his mother: a figure like a fertility goddess but with a thorn-studded tail curving gracefully over her head. The figure gazed at him with a feral grin. A joke between lovers, his father once explained, before telling him about the myth of the Sea Mother and her iron tail. "Because your mother was also an eater of men," he said with a mischievous grin.

Benji hadn't seen that grin in over a decade. He glanced away from the *tupilak* and saw a SynthMem device on the stand that once held a television. This he touched with his other hand, testing the polished feel of the plastic beneath his artificial skin, feeling the coolness of it a few seconds later than real skin would have. The SynthMem was the only new thing he noticed since the last time he'd gone hunting with his father.

A soapstone box rested next to it filled with labeled micro-discs of memory films. At the front of the stack, he found a thick bunch held together with a rubber band, the handwritten labels reduced to smudges: the ones reading his mother's name, "Opik," were faded and ghostly, as were the ones labeled with his own name. But he noticed other sections seemed freshly written, like the ones labelled "Arnauyq," his older brother who'd died before Benji was born.

He pulled out one of the illegible ones and inserted it into the SynthMem. A red laser shot from the ceiling projector onto the floor next to him, then fanned throughout the room. As it expanded, it revealed a scene colored by the crimson, flickering light of the laser. He saw the water of the inlet stretching out before him until it faded into the edge of the couch. A young boy dangled his feet off a dock while someone taller, with large, weathered hands, showed him how to bait a fishing line with a piece of meat. *Ptarmigan*, Benji remembered. *The bait was ptarmigan.*

Instinctively, Benji stretched his mechanical hand toward his father's holographic ones, then caught himself and reached with his good hand instead. He knew his father would have preferred it.

Benji eased himself into a rocking chair and listened as his father explained the particulars of patience and casting and asking permission to kiss a girl. He smiled and imagined the sun kissing his face pink as it had that day, the tang of the sea spray in his nose, and the splintery boards beneath his backside, boards that had long since washed into the sea.

After a moment, he realized he was crying and quickly removed the memory film. He snatched another disc at random and popped it in. His mother's face appeared with sparkling eyes and a sultry pout. But when she closed her eyes with a low hum and leaned into the hands cupping her cheeks, Benji hurried to shut it off.

On impulse, he picked up one of the "Arnauyq" discs, one of only seven. A small body appeared lying on the bed, his face pale, with eyes closed and looking too much like Benji's own at that age. The Arnauyq on the bed was young, around seven years old, and wrapped in animal skins up to his neck. Their father's hands, with the same crescent-shaped scar on the right thumb, picked up the boy's body, carefully pulling it close and tight to the chest. Benji saw the body carried out the back door of their house, knowing it wouldn't be through the front door so as not to cause bad luck for the hunters.

The body was carried a short way into the backyard, as close as possible to where Arnauyq was born, with the only movement being the gentle back-and-forth sway as their father walked. There was a hole in the ground, in the back next to the swing set, which was not rusted and weather-darkened the way Benji remembered it. This one was made of shiny blue metal with a long hole dug freshly into the earth next to it, beside the mound of loose earth that sat like a small mountain to one side. They laid the body into the hole, being careful, so careful, with the boy's head. The supporting hand, the one with the scar, caressed the boy's cheek with the backs of his fingers. Then family members stepped into view with shovels: his uncle replacing the dirt over the top of the body while his great aunt and mother laid large white stones like teeth over the fresh earth.

Occasionally, the hands belonging to Benji's father would pause their work to raise up to where his face must be. The hands would wipe first one side, then the other, and then resume the placing of stones. Finally, the work ceased when a small mound remained, the same mound Benji knew still lay beneath the crook of the slide that he'd played on as a child. He'd been told to leave the stones, to never touch them lest his brother's soul be disturbed in Quidlivun, the Land of the Moon, where only the purest of souls reside.

The only sounds were the scraping of shovels against the earth and of the Shaman in his fringed leather outfit intoning in Inuktitut and beseeching Sedna to cleanse their father's and mother's spirits for whatever offense they'd given her that required the life of their son.

Benji pulled out the disc with a shaking hand. He'd never known his brother, having been a baby at the time of the memory he'd just witnessed. But he knew nobody ever mentioned Arnauyq's name, at least not without a night of heavy drinking, and that his toys and clothes had always looked nearly new and hardly played with, despite being hand-me-downs.

Frowning, he pulled another of Arnauyq's discs. This showed a younger version of the boy, his brown eyes sparkling like stars as he concentrated on the task in front of him. His small pink tongue stuck out between his thin lips as he carefully carved a sliver from a knob of driftwood. The knife in his hand was overlarge, with a handle that would have better fit their father's hand.

"Is that for Benji?" their father asked, and Benji could hear the smile in his voice. The little boy nodded, and for a time Benji just watched as the first shape was whittled away. He recognized the line of the toy boat he'd loved as a child, lost to the ocean when the twine on it broke. He'd cried for days after losing it, always having assumed it had been carved by their father.

Now he knew better.

He popped in another disc from the stack with the smudged labels. On choppy water, this time, from the perspective of one in a kayak. Ahead, another kayak bobbed sideways as the water thrashed against it. For a moment, the memory was a silent film playing in the middle of the hut, and then the screaming faded in: his father's voice crying his name, yelling in Inuktitut instead of English in his panic. Benji saw himself as a teenager, flailing in the water and then sinking below it. Moments later, the projected image of the sea rose, appearing to flood the hut itself, as his father plunged in after him with his bone knife clenched in one fist.

But his father's memory lacked the sensation of the searing tug of the line as it tightened around his forearm or the feeling of the cord flaying his flesh; unconsciously, he clenched his prosthetic hand against the memory. It had been like dying, like the Sea Mother was claiming him for herself, dragging him down for an infinite kiss with lips of ice and salt.

It had taken Benji almost a year to get used to the new arm. But he never acclimated to the way his father avoided looking at it, except to cast guilty glances when he thought himself unobserved. While Benji returned to hunting with his father, he couldn't bring himself to go out on the water, and his father never asked.

He rose, his stomach rolling over like waves against the shore. From above the door frame, he plucked the oar, the one his father had wielded like an extension of his own arm. The wood was smooth and vaguely warm.

"Let's go, Papa," Benji murmured as he fit his prosthetic fingers into the grooves worn into the handle. "The Sea Mother calls."

OR EVERY MAN BE BLIND

BY JESSE ROWELL

CORA THE KODIAK, A BEAR TRAINED IN THE ART OF
DIVINATION, STOPPED OVERTURNING TAROT CARDS.
SHE CRANED HER NECK AS IF ANALYZING THE NIGHT
sky, grunted at a smudge of northern lights covering
a constellation, and scattered the cards with her
massive paw. La Luna and Le Pape danced in the
wind before vanishing in the dark.

"*Porca miseria!*" Cora's trainer swore as he picked
up the cards and wiped the dirt off with his apron.
"Our future is not in the cards tonight."

Italian or English, she understood neither. The
sounds of humans either soothed or prompted action,
and clouds in the sky had started to make her uneasy.
She had dreamt of driftwood circling above her and
branches crashing down on her head.

Cora's trainer shuffled the tarot cards back together
and walked her to her cage. Wisps of green snaked
above them through the mountains. Her muscles

seized, and she stopped. These weren't the same driftwood clouds from her dreams but something worse. She stood on her hind legs to sniff the air.

"*Siediti!*" the trainer warned.

Cora knew well enough what that sound meant as her trainer tugged on the twine around her neck. He senses danger, too, she thought. With a harrumph she swiped at the twine and lumbered away. Away from the mountains. Away from the strange green clouds.

They chased her through the night until she found a forest, or what remained of a forest. She burrowed beside the base of a burnt-out stump and looked up to watch emerald green glitter between charred silhouettes of branches. They made pleasing shapes like the ones she remembered, and she fell asleep under jeweled edges of tarot cards.

The northern lights ebbed, and the morning's gray corpse turned red with the promise of a new day. The charcoaled remains of a dead forest rose around her, not that she could remember what a living forest looked like. An unburned flank became her scratching post, and she moved her back up and down over its surface, leaving tufts of fur and scent on its bark.

She sniffed the air. No food here, but she felt a foreign feeling similar to hunger. She missed her trainer, that hairless bear who had watched her move tarot cards and rewarded her with bowls of stew. A strange, empty world opened up before her now with no human companion.

Hadn't there been another bear once? Something of a memory there. The heat he had generated. It lingered on her fur like sunshine. She felt life stirring inside her, a gestating urgency to find hibernation. But food first.

Cora had no memory of salmon, which hadn't existed in the wild for decades, but she caught scent of a fish fry several kilometers away. Instinct gripped her, a hunger more clawing than anything she could remember, and she pushed through the dead forest, toppling the husks of once majestic trees.

The land descended into scree, and she traversed a slurry of rocks, her claws breaking its shale into shards. A series of colorful flags and tents sat at the bottom of where smoke drifted up the hill. It enraged her senses, the colors of fruit mixing with the smells of plenty. She galloped toward the human habitation but stopped short upon seeing the glint of steel moving in the sun.

A human made of metal, spinning pinwheels for eyes, stood in front of a smoker as it turned fish. The thing looked human, exaggerated features where features were supposed to be, but mechanical like the useless things her trainer had toyed with late at night while she slept in her cage. Its eyes clicked, and it tilted its head to look at her.

"You seem lost, Ursa Major?" the robot asked. "I see twine tied around your neck. A domesticated bear in the age of extinction. What a remarkable find." It fiddled with one of the objects tied around its torso, a jar of broken glass. The jar clanked and rattled as it rebounded off its metal flank.

Cora sat on her haunches and watched people feel their way out of the tents, men and women smiling vacantly as they gazed at the sun. Docile and nonthreatening, her favorite kind of humans, the kind that gave her food for tricks, but there was something different about these people. After getting their fill of sunlight, they stumbled over each other toward the rattling sound and held out their hands. The robot fed them each with the patience of a mother.

"Children of the Sun," the robot announced as they nibbled at the pink flecks of flesh between translucent bones. "We are fortunate to have the bear constellation come down from heaven. Feel her fur, for she is pregnant and will bring us good fortune."

They felt at her with their fishy hands, smiling and mumbling to each other as they wiped grease on her fur. Cora didn't mind. She happily crunched on fish heads and fish tails the metal one had dumped in front of her. Juices ran down her chin.

"They like you, Ursa. If you agree to our rites of passage, we will keep you here and feed you every day, but you must gaze upon the sun. It is only after utter blindness that one sees the unseeable."

Cora looked up from the fish scraps and grunted agreeably. The sun-gazers' small hands scratched her itches. Their whispers threaded the air like wind.

Lulled, she rolled on her back for tummy rubs like her trainer used to give. The sun-gazers rubbed their magic bear's belly. She purred as she drifted into languor, her eyes closing over an orange sky with no clouds.

"The time approaches," the robot announced and led them back into their tents. A peaceful silence gave way to discordant humming, humans wailing from the interiors of their colorful walls. What strange sounds, she thought, and stood up to sniff the air.

"Don't fret, Ursa. Their prayers are starships piercing the firmament. Today will be another fine day for liftoff. For those who have given up. The rest of us will stay here to repair what is broken."

Cora did not understand the sun-gazers' humming, nor did she understand the robot's words of assurance, only that the dirt below her feet had started to shake. Imperceptible at first, and then concussive. Driftwood clouds erupted in the distance.

"Stay calm, Ursa." The volume of its voice rose. "There is no danger here. We are a safe distance away from the rockets. Distance is the commodity of the future. Distance to the stars. Distance from our burning planet."

Cora gauged the distance between the robot's torso and her claws, but before she could strike the air ripped apart. She snapped her jaw and charged. The tents collapsed. Sun-gazers flew into the air. She bellowed, and the clouds billowed back. People groped against the ground like helpless grubs. Their robot caregiver chased after her with commands to stop.

Contrails arced across the sky, some parallel and some intersecting, but far too many for Cora to comprehend the frequency of starships leaving Earth. When the rumbling had subsided, she couldn't stop running. She ran over cracked earth and fallow fields. The emptiness here felt wrong, a beige world with no humans left to attend to their machines.

The remains of a machine loomed in the distance, the tall skeleton of a launchpad's scaffolding silhouetted in the sun. It reminded her of the forest, and she ran toward it until she collapsed under its long shadow and panted for breath.

A clank and a rattle approached. "Ursa." The robot stood over her. "Despite your domestication, the consensus is that you should be put down. I protect the Children of the Sun, so this will be my task to bear."

The robot stood close enough for her to see the ephemera dangling off its torso. The jar of broken glass, a rusty key chain, and a set of bear claws. The claws matched her own, ivory, but larger, like those of a male Kodiak. She recognized the scent and remembered the heat he had generated. She growled.

"Now, now, big bear. I will make this painless, but you have to stay still."

Cora swung. The robot dodged faster than any human she could remember. She roared in frustration and lunged, but the robot was ready. It braced itself against the scaffolding and jabbed a sharp object deep into her shoulder. The flash of pain blinded her, her body convulsed, and she rolled to the side. Blood bloomed across her fur.

"Inaccuracy causes pain, and for that I am sorry. I missed your heart by sixty-eight centimeters. It's challenging to locate in your species. Now please stay still."

The robot measured the distance from her shoulder to her chest, pinwheel eyes clicking like insect wings, and it lifted its arm to drive the knife down into her. As it fell toward its target, the irresistible velocity of mechanical motion, the bear flung her paw back against the robot. Its chest crumpled, and effluent spurted through its cracks.

"I bleed," it said as it looked down at its body.

Cora mauled the robot until nothing of its previous form remained. The pain in her shoulder burned, but she didn't stop. She swept her paws over the ground and made a winding river of e-scrap that flowed from the launch pad to the field. Admiring her work, she sat in the shade and chewed on the chiffonade of the robot's face.

By evening she found the claws with the scent she recognized. She called out, a soft sound to find him, but no bear came out of the dark to reclaim his claws.

She remembered her trainer bringing him into their camp before he was taken away. That sunken feeling of loneliness returned, and all the happy memories hurt. She called out again, and upon hearing no response she plodded away from the launchpad.

She searched through the night for her trainer, the sun-gazers, or another bear. Anyone who could break this tired feeling of isolation. Her shoulder ached, and she paused occasionally to chew at the wound. It gave her respite from the bad feelings, but they always returned, and she resumed calling and searching.

Exhaustion clung to her like a dew she couldn't shake off. She slumped to the ground, eyelids sinking over an empty world. She dreamed more terrible dreams. Driftwood clouds and the sound of air being ripped apart. She awoke to the sound of voices.

"Cora," a man's voice said. "*Amica mia.*"

"She is a magnificent creature, isn't she?" a woman's voice asked, and then answered her own question. "Yes, truly magnificent."

The bear butted her head against her trainer and grunted happily. They wrestled, her pawing at his head and he pulling at her ears. She didn't mind that he poured a stinging liquid over her shoulder.

"Now for the real test," he said, setting a deck of tarot cards in front of her.

Cora looked up at the woman. She wore a bulky space suit, and her hair billowed out over her shoulders. The woman nodded, and the bear carefully flipped over three cards with an extended claw. La Stella, El Sole, and El Mondo looked up at them.

"Ahh, what a fortunate draw," her trainer said enthusiastically, as he was apt to do in front of customers. "The Star and The Sun mean you have a bright future, much success for interstellar travel."

"Does she really tell the future with those cards?" the woman asked.

"*Sì*, Claire. Every starship should have a fortune-telling bear."

"Good, then we have a deal." Claire extended her hand, and he shook it. "We need a domesticated bear for our flight toward a star in the Ursa Major constellation. Those poor fools who drew Leo will have a helluva time finding a lion. They'll never survive."

Claire let Cora sniff her before she rubbed her cheek. She murmured softly and tousled the bear's fur. "Who's the fuzzy-face? That's right, you're the fuzzy-face." She dropped colorful gummies on the ground for Cora to lap up. Sweet-tasting juices burst in her mouth. Each mouthful made her more sleepy. Darkness ate at the edges of her vision until all that remained was a void.

Cora dreamt no dreams. She didn't feel the shaking of liftoff, nor did she hear the roar of the spaceship escaping Earth's atmosphere. She slumbered in weightlessness until she fell into the pull of gravity and woke up in a forest.

Living trees untouched by fire, spruce and pine, rose above her. The water of a meandering stream disappeared into a hollow space at the edge of darkness. A mechanical breeze pushed fresh air over her face as robots toiled over soil and plants. The woman with billowing hair sat beside her.

"Hey, fuzzy-face. Did you sleep good?"

Cora harrumphed. Her groggy eyes tried to make sense of the forest biome spread out under a geodesic dome in outer space.

"Of course you did." Claire laughed. "With all those tranquilizers I fed you."

A waning Earth rose above the trees. Cora reflexively extended a practiced claw to overturn a tarot card where no card sat, and she dropped her paw back to the ground. The blue thing spun out of sight, and stars appeared in its place. The woman pointed at a cluster of stars and talked about Ursa Major, the promise of new worlds to colonize with new life. The bear looked instead at a fallen tree covered in emerald green moss and the inviting space underneath it.

Instinct told Cora that she should crawl into the den, escape the terrifying emptiness outside the dome. Escape back into sleep. But for a moment, she remembered Earth. The quiet moments when it seemed like life might recover. That had been something worth fighting for, lost somewhere in a place and time she could not comprehend.

ABOUT THE AUTHORS

DELANEY N. BROWN CURRENTLY ATTENDS FLORIDA State University, where she studies creative writing and works on her university's literary magazine, the Kudzu Review. This is her first publication.

LANE CHASEK IS THE AUTHOR OF A NOVEL, AN experimental biography, and a few books of poetry. His work has appeared or is forthcoming in *Denver Quarterly*, *McSweeney's*, *North American Review*, and many other publications. Along with writing, Lane also plays the harmonica.

DANIELLE DAVIS (SHE/HER) IS A LIAR, A CHEATER AT cards, and a misrememberer of song lyrics: only two of these are true. Her horror and dark fantasy have appeared in *The Santa Barbara Literary*

Journal, Andromeda Spaceways Magazine, and 40+ anthologies. An active contributor to Writer Unboxed, she is also a member of Horror Writers of America (HWA). You can find her on most social media platforms under the handle LiteraryEllyMay and at www.literaryellymay.com.

FAITH ANN GUPTILL LIVES IN WASHINGTON STATE, enjoying the rain with her two horses, Gracie and Monsta', and a German Shepard named Lux. Her inspiration comes from her many adventures, the people she has met, and her grandmother's love and wisdom. This year, her short stories have been published in the *MockingOwl Roost* and *WordPeace.* She was also a finalist in the Canopus Award for Excellence in Interstellar Writing, plus landed on the shortlist for the Art of Unity Creative Award. Impressed by a Michelangelo quote, "The greater danger for most of us lies not in setting our aim too high and falling short, but in setting our aim too low, and achieving our mark," she hovers at her desk typing out her stories in hopes to encourage other to cherish each day and aim for the stars.

REMI MARTIN IS A WRITER OF SCIENCE FICTION FROM Derbyshire in the UK. He has stories in *F&SF* and *Hexagon Magazine,* among other places, and is excited to be part of another *Ab Terra* anthology. If you wanted to read more, you'd find another one of his stories in *Ab Terra 2022*.

AMY MATTHEWSON'S CREATIVE WORK HAS APPEARED in *The Terry Project* and *Ricepaper* magazine. She is a historian by profession and interested in cross-cultural relations in the nineteenth and early twentieth century. Her book, *Cartooning China: Punch, Power, & Politics in the Victorian Era* was published by Routledge in 2022.

STEPHEN NOTHUM IS A FICTION WRITER AND LEARNING designer based in Eugene, Oregon. Stephen's work focuses on themes of pop culture, education, perceptions, mental health, social issues, and the concept of reality. His writing has been featured in *HASH Journal, The Bookends Review, Utah English Journal,* and *Zoetic Press*. Stephen has presented at conferences at both state and national levels on writing, writing education, and reading. His debut short story collection, *Teething and Other Tales from the American Dystopia*, released in December 2023.

MARKA RIFAT'S WRITTEN AND VISUAL WORK HAS WON awards and appears in over fifty North American, British, and Australian collections. In 2024, she was commended in the Oxford Poetry Library's inaugural competition. Recent publications include a poem in an anthology on place and belonging, three poems in *Dreich*, a photograph and poem in *The French Literary Review*, and a story in the final edition of the John Byrne Award website. Marka lives in Scotland and writes stories, poetry, essays, plays and articles, as well as producing drawings and photographs.

CHRIS ROBINSON LIVES IN ATLANTA WITH HIS SPOUSE, a pug, and three-quarters of a cat. A writer and student of science fiction, he is currently seeking representation for his debut novel while revising his second. When he's not writing, you can find him playing bass in local queercore powerhouse, ozello.

JESSE ROWELL (HE/HIM) IS AN AWARD-WINNING science fiction author whose work explores naturalism, technology, and the human condition. He can be found at https://jesserowell.com.

J. RILEY SHORT WAS BORN AND RAISED IN LIMA, OHIO, a small city in Northwestern Ohio best known for building both the M1 Abrams tank and the Shay locomotive. He lives there to this day with his calico cat, Denna. He loves to write speculative science fiction focusing on how advancing technology might affect the lives and culture of average people in the not-so-distant future. He also dabbles in writing fantasy when he's in the mood for swords and dragons. He graduated with a bachelor of arts in English literature from The Ohio State University at Lima, where he served as an assistant editor on the debut of their undergraduate literary journal *Asterism*, now the *Hog Creek Hardin Literary Journal*, in 2017. He is currently helping students gain access to Federal student aid as a financial aid officer at a small technical college in his hometown. His appearance in *Ab Terra 2023* is the first time one of his stories has been published.

ABOUT THE EDITORS

YEN OOI IS A WRITER AND EDITOR—2023 HUGO AWARD finalist—whose works explore cultural storytelling and its effects on identity. She is obsessed with science fiction, where she excavates stories to expose and explore permutations of culture across the genre. Yen is author of *Rén: The Ancient Chinese Art of Finding Peace and Fulfilment*, narrative designer on *Road to Guangdong*, as well as author of *Sun: Queens of Earth* (novel) and *A Suspicious Collection of Short Stories and Poetry* (collection). When she hasn't got her head in a book, Yen also lectures, mentors, and plays the viola.

DAWN OSTLUND WRITES STORIES ABOUT technology's incursion on the rituals and traditions of different cultures around the world. She holds an MA in Politics, Media and Performance and an MA in Creative Writing. She lives in Los Angeles and works as an editor and proofreader.